What Would a DUKE DO?

Seductive Scoundrels, Book Four

COLLETTE CAMERON

Blue Rose Romance®
Portland, Oregon

Sweet-to-Spicy Timeless Romance®

WHAT WOULD A DUKE DO?
Seductive Scoundrels

Cover Design by: Kim Killion

Blue Rose Romance®
8420 N Ivanhoe # 83054
Portland, Oregon 97203

ISBN Paperback: 9781954307599
ISBN eBook: 9781954307582
www.collettecameron.com

“I could have loved you, Maxwell.”

I could have loved you too, my darling Gabby.

Daughters of Desire (Scandalous Ladies)
A Lady, A Kiss, A Christmas Wish
Coming soon in the series!
No Lady for the Lord
Love Lessons for a Lady
His One and Only Lady

The Honorable Rogues®
A Kiss for a Rogue
A Bride for a Rogue
A Rogue's Scandalous Wish
To Capture a Rogue's Heart
The Rogue and the Wallflower
A Rose for a Rogue

The Blue Rose Regency Romances:
The Culpepper Misses
The Earl and the Spinster
The Marquis and the Vixen
The Lord and the Wallflower
The Buccaneer and the Bluestocking
The Lieutenant and the Lady

Highland Heather Romancing a Scot
Triumph and Treasure
Virtue and Valor
Heartbreak and Honor
Scandal's Splendor
Passion and Plunder
Seductive Surrender
A Yuletide Highlander

Castle Brides

The Viscount's Vow

Highlander's Hope

The Earl's Enticement

Heart of a Highlander (*prequel to Highlander's Hope*)

Seductive Scoundrel's

A Diamond for a Duke

Only a Duke Would Dare

A December with a Duke

What Would a Duke Do?

Wooed by a Wicked Duke

Duchess of His Heart

Never Dance with a Duke

Earl of Wainthorpe

Earl of Scarborough

The Debutante and the Duke

Wedding her Christmas Duke

Earl of Keyworth

Coming soon in the series!

How to Win A Duke's Heart

Loved by a Dangerous Duke

When a Duke Loves a Lass

Boxed Sets

Lords in Love

The Honorable Rogues® Books 1-3

The Honorable Rogues® Books 4-6

Seductive Scoundrels Series Books 1-3

Seductive Scoundrels Series Books 4-6

The Blue Rose Regency Romances:

The Culpepper Misses Series 1-2

To my fabulous, loyal readers, especially my beta babes: SC, TN, DF, BSB, FM, TE, KS

Thank you!

Prologue

December 1809

Ridgewood Court, Essex England

Humming beneath her breath, Gabriella Breckensole practically skipped down the stairs on her way to meet the other female houseguests to make kissing boughs and other festive decorations. The past few days had been a whirlwind of activity, as her hostess, Theadosia, the Duchess of Sutcliffe and one of her dearest friends, hosted a Christmastide house party, the likes of which Essex had never witnessed before.

The event was made all that much more enjoyable by the presence of Maxwell Woolbright, the Duke of

Pennington. Since Gabriella and her twin sister had returned from finishing school almost two years ago, she'd encountered him at a few gatherings. He was quite the most dashing man she'd ever met, and despite being far above her station, she thrilled whenever he directed his attention her way.

Descending the last riser, she puzzled for a moment. Where were the ladies to meet? The drawing room, the floral salon, or the dining room? Forehead scrunched, she pulled her mouth to the side and started toward the drawing room. Halfway there, she remembered they were to meet in the slightly larger dining room. She spun around and marched the other direction, passing the impressive library, its door slightly ajar.

"Harold Breckensole will pay for what he's done," a man declared in an angry, gruff voice.

Gabriella halted mid-step, her stomach plunging to her slippered feet. She swiftly looked up and down the vacant corridor before tip-toeing to the cracked doorway. Who spoke about her grandfather with such hostility?

Breath held, she peeked through the narrow opening. The Dukes of Sutcliffe, Pennington, and Sheffield stood beside the fireplace, facing each other.

Pennington held a glass of umber-colored spirits in one hand as he stared morosely into the capering flames. "I shall reclaim Hartfordshire Court. I swear."

"You say the estate was once part of the unentailed part of the duchy?" Sutcliffe asked, concern forming a line between his eyebrows.

Pennington tossed back a swallow of his drink. "Yes. It belonged to my grandmother's family for generations, and after what I've recently learned, I mean to see it restored to the ducal holdings, come hell or high water. And I'll destroy Breckensole too."

Slapping a hand over her mouth, she backed away, shaking her head as stinging tears slid from the corners of her eyes.

Oh, my God. She'd been halfway to falling in love with a man bent on revenge of some sort. Gabriella jutted her chin up, angrily swiping at her cheeks. The Duke of Pennington had just become her enemy.

1

Late March 1810

Colechester, Essex, England

"Miss Breckensole, what an unexpected… pleasure," a man drawled in a cultured voice, the merest hint of laughter coloring his melodious baritone.

Unexpected and wholly unwelcome.

Gabriella froze in her admiration of Nicolette Twistleton's adorable pug puppy, and barely refrained from gnashing her teeth. She knew full well who stood behind her. The odious, arrogant—*annoying as Hades*—Maxwell, Duke of Pennington. His delicious cologne wafted past her nostrils, and she let her eyelids drift half shut as she ordered her heart to resume its regular cadence.

He didn't know what she'd discovered about him. That he was a dishonorable, deceiving blackguard behind his oh, so charming demeanor. And he meant to destroy her grandfather. That knowledge bolstered her courage and settled her erratic pulse.

One midnight eyebrow arched questioningly; Nicolette threw her a harried glance before dipping into a curtsy. "Your Grace."

Gabriella hadn't confided in Nicolette. Hadn't confided in anyone as to why she disliked him so very much. Quashing her irritation at his appearance and his daring to greet her as if they were the greatest of friends, she schooled her features into blandness before turning and sinking into the expected deferential greeting. "Duke."

He bowed; his strong mouth slanted into his usual half-mocking smile.

"What brings you to town?" He glanced around. "Your sister or grandmother aren't with you? Or an abigail either?" A hint of disapproval edged his observation. "Did you come with Miss Twistleton?"

Beast. Who was he to question her conduct? She wasn't accountable to him.

"No, I am here with my mother." Nicolette cast Gabriella another bewildered glance. "She's in the milliner's."

Surely, he was aware, as was the whole of Colechester, that a lady's maid was an unnecessary expense, according to Gabriella's grandfather. That the duke so offhandedly and publicly made mention of the deficiency angered and chagrined her.

Pennington turned an expectant look upon her. As if he were entitled to have an answer, because, after all, *he* was the much sought-after Duke of Pennington.

Edging her chin upward, Gabriella clutched her packages tighter, one of which was her twin's birthday present. She saved for months to be able to surprise Ophelia with the mazurine blue velvet cloak.

"Grandmama is unwell, and Ophelia stayed home to care for her." She wouldn't offer him further explanation.

"I am truly sorry to hear that. May I have my physician call upon her?" he asked, all solicitousness, even going so far as to lower his brows as if he truly cared. A concern she knew to be feigned given what she'd overheard at the Duke and Duchess of Sutcliffe's Christmastide house party last December.

"That's not necessary. She was seen by one only last week." My, she sounded positively unaffected. The epitome of a self-possessed gently-bred young woman.

Inside, she fumed at his forwardness.

How she wanted to rail at him. To tell him precisely what she thought of his nefarious scheme. Why did he—*conceited, handsome rakehell*—have to be in Colechester today too? He promptly turned her much-anticipated afternoon outing sour. Freshly cut lemon or gooseberry face-puckering, attitude-ruining sour.

And why he insisted upon trying to speak to her at every opportunity, she couldn't conceive. Three months ago, and the few unfortunate occasions they'd come across each other since, she'd made her feelings perfectly clear—to-the-point-of-rudeness-clear.

She'd heard him vow to the Dukes of Sheffield and Sutcliffe that *come hell or high water*—Pennington's very sternly muttered words—he'd reclaim the lands that had once been an unentailed part of the duchy. Lands that had belonged to his grandmother's family for generations.

Property, which included her beloved home, Hartfordshire Court. A holding that Grandpapa had purchased, fair and square, from the duke's own degenerate grandfather decades before and which, with hard work and industry, had made the estate prosperous.

"Mama is so very pleased you are to attend our musical assembly, Your Grace," Nicolette blurted. As if sensing the stilted silence and not understanding the reason why, but wanting to defuse the tangible awkwardness.

Unable to contain her disbelief, Gabriella sent him a quick glance from beneath her lashes. *He is to attend? Of all the dashed rotten luck.* He rarely remained at his country seat past mid-March. London held far more appeal to a man of the world like him, and truth be told, she had anticipated—*needed*—a few months' reprieve from his presence.

She and Ophelia were to attend as well, but now she no longer anticipated her first social foray other than tea in two months as she had but a minute ago.

Nicolette shifted the puppy and received a wet tongue on the cheek for her efforts. "No licking, Bella," she admonished whilst rubbing the pup behind her ears. "It's also Gabriella's birthday that day," she offered with an impish twinkle in her eye. "She'll be one and twenty."

Gabriella shot her a quelling glance. The world—*he*—didn't need to know she was practically on the shelf with no prospects, save spinsterhood.

"I quite look forward to the entertainment." Insincerity rang in his tone as he gave a gracious nod and continued staring at Gabriella. "And also, to wish you a happy day, Miss Breckensole." The latter held a note of authenticity. He flicked his gaze down the street, seeming uncharacteristically uncertain. "Ladies, would you join me for a cup of chocolate or coffee?"

The Prince's Coffee House was but four doors down and acclaimed not only for its hot beverages, but ambiance and scrumptious pastries. Not that Gabriella had ever sampled either.

She'd wanted to, but Grandpapa frowned upon eating in the village. A waste of good coin, he grumbled.

Nicolette shook her head, no genuine regret shadowing her face. After being jilted, she bore disdain for every male, save her brother, the Earl of Scarborough. "I fear Mama is expecting me inside. I only came outside for Bella's sake."

"And I must return home straightaway." Gabriella signaled her driver with a flick of her wrist and slant of her head. She'd finished her shopping before bumping into Nicolette and the newest addition to the Twistleton household.

Amid a chorus of creaks and groans, her grandfather's slightly lopsided and dated coach pulled alongside her. Jackson, the groomsman, climbed down and after three rigorous attempts, managed to lower the steps. She passed him her parcels, which he promptly placed inside the conveyance.

"Please allow me." The duke stepped forward and offered his hand to assist her inside.

While she wanted to give him the cut by refusing to accept his offer, Nicolette was sure to interrogate her as to why she'd been so rude the next time they met. A year ago, even three months ago, Gabriella would've been overjoyed at his attention. Now, he was her enemy. A handsome, dangerous, cunning, and unpredictable nemesis.

As lightly as she was able, she placed her fingertips atop his palm and entered the rickety out of fashion forty-year-old coach. Lips melded, she studiously disregarded the alarming jolt of sensation zipping up her arm at his touch. She should feel nothing but contempt for him and most assuredly entertain no carnal attraction.

The duke didn't immediately close the door behind her. His gaze probed hers for a long sliver of a moment, and suddenly the coach became very confining. And hot. She waved her hand before her face, having left her fan at home. "Might I call upon you tomorrow?" *Is he utterly daft?* "Perhaps we might take a ride? Naturally, Miss Ophelia is welcome too."

That latter seemed more of an after-thought. He knew she couldn't ride out alone with him, and he was mad as a Bedlam guest if he truly believed she'd willingly spend time in his company.

Gabriella met his gaze straight on. Something undefinable shadowed the depths of his unusual eyes—one green and one blue. "I must decline, Your Grace. I also must ask you, once again, to direct your attentions elsewhere. I am not now, nor will I ever be, receptive to them."

If she never spoke to him again, it would be too soon.

Did he really think just because he was a duke and she was the lowly granddaughter of a gentleman-farmer, she'd jump at the opportunity to spend time in his company?

You did at one time. And suffered a broken heart when his true character became evident.

Not. Anymore. Never again. Not when she knew his true motivation for seeking her company. How much her feelings had changed for him these past months.

At once his striking countenance grew shuttered, his high cheekbones more pronounced with… Anger? Disappointment? "We, shall see, *chérie*. We shall see."

"What, precisely, do you mean by that?" Something very near dread clogged her throat, and the words came out husky rather than terse as she'd intended.

Instead of answering, he offered an enigmatic smile and doffed his hat, the afternoon sunlight glinting on his raven hair. "Good day."

We, shall see, chérie. We shall see.

His words replaying over and over in her mind, she remained immobile, her focus trained on his retreating form until he disappeared into the Pony and Pint instead of The Prince's Coffee House. At one time, she'd fancied herself enamored of him. She'd been flattered he'd turned his ducal attention on her: a simple country girl without prospects.

Firmly stifling those memories and the associated emotions, she tapped the roof. "Home. Jackson, and do hurry. Grandmama needs her medicines."

And I need to put distance between myself and the Duke of Pennington. Because even though she knew the truth, a tiny part of her heart yet ached for him, and she loathed herself for that weakness.

Two hours later shivering and briskly rubbing her arms, Gabriella bent forward to peer out the coach window again.

Tentatively probing her head, she winced. The knot from smacking her noggin on the side of the vehicle when the axle snapped hadn't grown any larger. Neither did it bleed. Nonetheless, the walnut-sized lump ached with the ferocity of a newly trapped tiger. A superbly large, sharp-toothed, and foul-tempered beast.

"Really," she muttered, exasperated and uncharacteristically cross from hunger, cold, and the painful bump. "Whatever can be taking Jackson so long to return? Hartsfordshire Court isn't so very blasted far."

Less than two miles she estimated after another glance at the familiar green meadow sloping to the winding river beyond. The recent rains caused the brown-tinged water to run high and spill over its banks, as it did nearly every spring. In the summer, the lush grasslands fed Grandpapa's famed South Devon cattle on one side, and their neighbor, the Duke of Pennington's fluffy black-faced sheep on the other.

An uncharitable thought about the distinction between the keen intelligence of cows and sheep's lack of acumen tried to form, but she squelched it. It wasn't the poor sheep's fault she couldn't abide their owner.

After repeatedly assuring her hesitant coachman she would be perfectly fine until he returned with the seldom-used phaeton, Jackson had swiftly stridden away. Not, however, without turning to work his worried gaze over her, the team, and the disabled coach's crippled wheel thrice. Each time, she donned a smile wide enough to crack her cheeks and made a shooing motion for him to continue on.

For pity's sake. She wasn't one of those silly,

simpering misses afraid the hem of her skirt might become dusty or who shrieked hysterically upon a cobweb brushing her gloves or cheek. So long as the resident eight-fuzzy-legged spider had *long* since removed itself to a new home.

If it weren't for her impractical footwear, Gabriella would've walked as well. But, she'd no wish for bruised feet or the lecture certain to follow from dear Grandpapa about the cost of replacing ruined slippers. And that would probably produce another discourse about unnecessary trips to Colechester for what he deemed nonsensical fripperies.

Perhaps they were absurd to a man given to wearing the same staid suit and shoes for the past five years as Grandpapa had been. But Ophelia's birthday present wasn't a silly frippery. Neither were Grandmama's medicine nor the chemises for Gabriella and her sister frivolous expenses. It had been three years since anyone had purchased new undergarments.

With her leftover pin money—one half a crown every month—Gabriella had purchased the beloved hunch-shouldered curmudgeon his favorite blend of pipe tobacco. Oh, he'd grumble and grouse over the wasteful spending, but she hadn't a doubt she'd earn a kiss upon her forehead before he shuffled off to enjoy a pipe and a tot in his fusty study amongst his even fustier tomes.

A wry smile quirked her mouth.

Did Grandpapa use the same tobacco five times as he insisted Grandmama do with tea leaves? Anything to save a penny or two. The Breckensoles didn't enjoy neat lumps of white sugar in their tea either, but rather the golden-brown nubs chiseled from a cheaper hard-as-a-blasted-boulder loaf. Since they never—truly never—had guests for tea or for any other occasion for that matter, there was no need to feel a trifle embarrassed at the economy.

She ran a gloved finger over the lumpy parcel containing the umber-brown bottles for her grandmother. A month ago, a nasty cough had settled in Grandmama's lungs, and she couldn't shake the ailment.

Gabriella's current discomfort tugged her meandering musings back to her immediate situation.

For all of two seconds—fine, mayhap three—she'd considered riding one of the horses still harnessed to the coach home. But that would've required hiking her gown knee-high and riding astride. Even she daren't that degree of boldness.

Nonetheless, on days she yearned to toss aside society's and her strict grandparents' constraints, she *might've* been known to sneak a horse from the stables and ride along the river: bonnet-free and skirts rucked most inappropriately high. Oh, the freedom was wondrous, though the tell-tale freckles that were wont to sprout upon her nose usually gave her recklessness away.

Her grandparents never lectured, but their silent disapproval was sufficient to quell her hoydenish ways. For a week or two.

The carriage made an eerie noise; the way a vehicle sounded in the throes of death. *If* a vehicle were capable of such a thing. Another juddering crack followed as the damaged side wedged deeper into the dirt.

She let loose a softly-sworn oath no respectable

woman ought to know, let alone utter aloud as she grabbed the seat to keep from tumbling onto the floor. A labored groan and a piercing creak followed on the heels of her crude vulgarity, and a five-inch-long jagged crack split the near window.

"Blast and damn."

A new chill skidded down her spine as she mentally braced herself for Grandpapa's intense displeasure. He'd be aggravated about the damage to the coach, but more so about the cost to repair it. A frugal, self-made man, he was as reluctant to part with a coin as he was to leave Hartfordshire Court. Others who didn't know him well called him stingy and miserly.

In the fifteen years since coming to live at Hartfordshire, Gabriella could count on two hands the number of times either grandparent had left the estate. She would shrivel up and die if forced to stay there months on end.

Yet, her hermit-like grandparents had been diligent to assure she and her sister never lacked for company or social interactions. They'd even conceded to send the twins to finishing school. At no little cost either. What a juxtaposition. Her grandparents eschewed all things social, but she and her sister craved the routs, soirees, balls, picnics, musical parties, and all else that guaranteed a superior assemblage.

One troublesome, unignorable fact remained unaddressed, however. Grandpapa had never spoken of a dowry for either of them. They'd never wanted for necessities, but Gabriella suspected his pockets weren't as flush as he'd have his family believe.

Her heart gave a queer pang. It wasn't exactly worry or distress. But neither was the peculiar feeling frustration or disappointment. Nevertheless, it left her unsettled. Discontent and restless. Disconcerted about what her future might entail. Ophelia's too.

As improbable as it was, except for splurging on the matched team and phaeton, her grandfather had been noticeably less inclined to spend money after the twins returned home two years ago. Now, almost one and twenty, their aging grandparents' health beginning to fail, and their neighbor, the mercenary Duke of Pennington, bent on stealing Hartsfordshire Court from them, Gabriella fretted about what would happen to her sister if neither one of them married and soon.

There weren't exactly men—noble or otherwise—scurrying to form a queue to court either of them. Or to dance with them at assemblies or request romantic strolls through opulent gardens. No posies, sweets, or poems found their way to the house's front door on a regular basis either. On *any* basis, for that matter.

Oh, the country gentlemen were kind and polite enough. Indeed, some aristocrats and gentry—even a rogue or two—had been downright charming and flirtatious. More than one had hinted they'd very much like to pursue an immoral liaison. But the simple truth was as obvious as a giraffe's purple tongue sampling pea soup in the dining room. Dowerless, Gabriella's and Ophelia's prospects were few.

Nonexistent, truth to tell.

For one horrid, ugly fact couldn't be overlooked: a woman without a dowry, no matter how refined, immaculately fitted out, or proficient in French, Latin, Spanish, painting, playing the pianoforte—or the violin in Gabriella's case—and managing a household she might be, without the lure of a marriage settlement to entice a respectable suitor, such an unfortunate lady was labeled an undesirable.

And much like other hapless women in the same ill-fated predicament, spinsterhood, dark and foreboding, loomed on the horizon, a slightly terrifying fate for any young woman.

Which made the duke's interest in her all the more questionable. He couldn't possibly have honorable intentions.

She pursed her mouth, drawing her eyebrows into a taut line. Barbaric, this business of bribing a man with money, land, and the good Lord only knew what else to take a woman to wife. Why couldn't love be enough?

Like Theadosia and Sutcliffe? Or her maternal cousin Everleigh and the Duke of Sheffield? Or even Jemmah and Jules, the Duke and Duchess of Dandridge? Once not so long ago, Gabriella had yearned for that kind of love. Had dared to hope she might've found it, but the object of her affections had turned out to be a colossal rat.

Unfortunately, such was the nature of the Marriage Mart. Without dowries, Gabriella and her twin could look forward to caring for their grandparents into their dotage rather than marry and have families. Their lack of suitors could be laid at Society's silk-clad feet. Strictures, along with a goodly portion of greed and hunger for power, dictated most matches. That, regrettably, was an indisputable fact.

Something uncomfortable and slightly terrifying, much like melancholy, turned over in her breast and swirled in her stomach. To distract herself from her somber reflections, she inspected the lonely road once more.

The fading afternoon sun filtering through the towering evergreen treetops on the other side of the deserted track confirmed dusk's dark cloak and chill would blanket the countryside soon. For at least the sixth time in the past hour, Gabriella examined the dainty timepiece pinned to her spencer.

She frowned and gave it a little shake. Was the deuced thing working?

Yes, the big hand shifted just then. She huffed out

a small petulant sigh, for she recognized her own impatience.

Where the devil was Jackson, for pity's sake? Had something waylaid him? *Obviously.* Yes, but what? The unbidden thoughts agitated her already heightened nerves. Nerves that had been fraught since departing the village earlier.

Angered anew at Pennington's audacity, she pressed her lips into an irritated line and fisted her hands. Only he had the ability to make her so peeved. *Bloody, greedy bounder. By Jove, didn't he have enough? Why must he covet what we have too?*

Chartworth Hall was an immense estate boasting some two-thousand acres, a mansion—more castle than house—a hunting lodge, a dower house, embarrassingly massive and full stables, and numerous other outbuildings.

Why the duke focused on Hartfordshire's acres and seventeen-room residence, quite desperately in need of refurbishing and restoration, made no sense at all. She didn't know the particulars of the sale. Neither did she understand how the unentailed property came to be adjacent to the entailed lands, but she didn't give a fig.

What she *did* care about was the duke's callousness. His insensitivity and cold-heartedness. He hadn't a thought for any of the Breckensoles, of displacing them from their home. Oh, no. His only concern was how to cheat Grandpapa out of his property and to expand the already enormous ducal holdings.

By God, she wouldn't permit it. She would not.

2

Drumming her fingertips atop her thigh, Gabriella huffed out another frustrated breath. Ophelia was the patient twin. The sensible twin. The good-natured, genial twin. The one capable of tempering tart retorts and painting a benign mien upon her features.

Far too frequently, Gabriella spoke her mind and responded with emotion rather than reason. Alternating tapping her toes on the sloping floor, one foot then the next, she put a hand to her hollow middle and moistened her lower lip. She was rather parched too.

Memory of the meat pies and other savory foods' aromas wafting from the lodging house and The Prince's Coffee House caused her stomach to protest loudly. *We've plenty of food and refreshment at Hartfordshire Court. No sense wasting good coin.* Grandpapa's admonishment replayed through her mind.

She still hadn't informed her grandparents of Pennington's devious plan. She couldn't fathom a legal way he could regain the estate, and therefore, rather than cause the elderly pair an upset, she kept the knowledge to herself.

When the need arose—*pray God it never would*—she'd tell all. But until that time, the tall debonair duke with his shock of midnight hair and unusual eyes beneath slashing brows the same hue as his hair, wasted his time directing his attention toward her. She, alone, must protect her family from that craven's cunning and scheming.

In fact, she'd taken to carrying a small dagger in her boot or reticle. Just in case…Well, she didn't know exactly what. But far better to be prepared than caught unawares. She also knew how to wield a fan, a hat pin, and even a parasol as an improvised weapon should the need arise. Nicolette firmly believed every woman should be able to defend herself, and Gabriella agreed wholeheartedly.

Her ability to fend off an attacker was another reason she'd been comfortable sending Jackson for assistance. Besides, rarely did anyone travel this isolated length of road. Only Hartfordshire Court, Pennington's palatial country seat, and a seldom used shortcut connecting the main route to London lay this far along the remote track.

Flopping back against the pale blue velvet squabs, she folded her arms and wrinkled her nose.

How could she ever have thought the Duke of Pennington amusing or charming? *Enthralling. Fascinating. Wholly extraordinary.* His black-lashed eyes *were* quite extraordinary. Never before had she seen anyone with two different colored eyes. They enhanced the air of mystery surrounding him. As if he were privy to a secret no one else knew. She'd seen it in the way he observed her through his heavy-lidded, smoldering eyes.

A little rush of exhilaration tingled in her blood.

Heavy-lidded? Smoldering? My God.

What in the world had come over her? Surely it must be hunger or the knock to her head. Either or perhaps both had made her dizzy and fanciful.

What a good thing she discovered his true colors before she'd permitted her schoolgirl *tendre* to foolishly become something more. Now, however, she knew better than to trust his cheerful demeanor and too-alluring-for-her-good smile. All of his attention and murmured compliments had all been a calculated ruse to get near her and use her as a means to rob her grandparents of their home. Oh, how she longed to plant him a facer or challenge him to pistols or swords.

She wasn't such a refined lady that either choice wasn't an option.

Her grandparents would be horrified to know, but she and Ophelia had learned fencing, how to shoot pistols, and even how to deliver a precisely-aimed blow with their fists. All thanks to their many visits and overnight stays with her dear friend, Nicolette.

Gabriella tapped her chin with her forefinger. Mayhap she should ask Nicolette how to discourage a gentleman's attention. After being jilted a mere day before her wedding, her friend had perfected snubbing men to a fine art. To the point of cruelty at times. Nicolette also possessed an assortment of naughty romance novels, which she freely shared with her friends.

Or perchance, Gabriella should enlist her cousin Everleigh or their mutual friend Theadosia for help. The duchesses could discretely question their husbands about what types of things were certain to put Pennington off the chase.

What surely must be a crafty smile tipped her mouth.

Why, yes. Why hadn't she considered that sooner?

Shifting uncomfortably, she eyed the wispy ferns and underbrush crowding the tree trunks. Nature called with ever-increasing urgency.

Finally, when another impatient glare to her timepiece revealed ten more minutes had inched past, she could wait no longer. With some difficulty, and only by pressing her shoulder forcefully into the stubborn panel, she managed to shove the door open then hopped to the ground. In the looming twilight, a magnificent stag stood near the river. Ebony eyes wary and ears twitching, he observed her, the tips of his mighty antlers obscured in the gloaming light.

If only she had her pencils and sketch pad, she might've drawn him, and she'd have had something to pass the time as well. She must remember to bring them next time, for one never knew when an opportunity might arise that she'd want to record on paper. Apparently deciding she posed him no threat, the stag lowered his head to the shimmering water.

The horses, a striking matched pair of grays right down to their black manes and tails, flicked those impressive tails and shifted their feet. No doubt they longed for their warm stalls and a bucket of oats to happily munch upon.

She yearned for a hot bath liberally sprinkled with jasmine, lavender, and lemongrass-scented oil—her own creation since perfume was an expense Grandpapa disallowed. A bowl of Mrs. McCandish's sumptuous cock-a-leekie soup, and an equally hot toddy, generously laced with whisky wouldn't go amiss either.

"Brrr."

Shivering, Gabriella rubbed the dark green velvet covering her arms again as she carefully studied the narrow, rutted track first in one direction then the other. When she'd left the house this afternoon, the temperature had been quite warm for March. Since she traveled directly to Colechester and back, she hadn't believed a cloak necessary.

Neither was there a lap robe in the drafty coach. Grandpapa claimed the moths and vermin would feast upon it. One didn't argue with him or point out that the robe might be stored inside the house until needed.

Always the more practical sister, Ophelia's advice from earlier today rang in Gabriella's ears. "Gabby, you really ought to at least take a shawl or mantle. You know how quickly the weather can turn ugly this time of year. We don't need you falling ill as well."

In her typical impetuous way, Gabriella had ignored her sister's warning, more fool she. Especially, if night fell before, she was rescued. It surely appeared as if it would.

That miserable thought coiled in her empty belly.

It was one thing to think oneself daring and independent in daylight and another thing entirely when darkness blacker than a moonless night descended upon the countryside… *This* oh, so very isolated particular spot of countryside to be precise.

Despite her impulsive inclinations, she'd never pretended to be an audacious, adventurous sort. With each passing minute, real concern for Jackson grew. As did the unpleasant realization that she very well may have to spend the night huddled in the coach or trod home in the dark.

Alone.

With wild, *hungry* creatures meandering about.

Each alternative held as much appeal as kissing Pennington. *Kissing Pennington?* Good heavens, where did that odious thought come from? *Is it truly odious?*

Yes, she very sternly chided her romping imagination. *Of course it is.* Everything to do with him was disagreeable, the charlatan. Pretending to be her friend and paying her marked attention all the while plotting to steal her home.

She'd sooner pull every hair from her head than touch her mouth to his.

Liar, chided an annoying voice in her mind. Thoroughly vexed, she admonished the voice to shut up.

After giving each gelding a pet on his withers, she adjusted her askew bonnet more firmly upon her head. She retied the ribbons beneath what she considered a too-strong jaw for a female. Grandmama, a twinkle in her eyes, declared it was no such thing. It was merely Gabriella's tendency to jut her chin out in obstinacy that made her jawline appear prominent.

Considering her grandmother's penchant for doing the exact same thing, Gabriella was hard put to argue against her jesting.

Hands on her hips, a frown turning the corners of her mouth downward, she weighed her options. Stay here or walk home? Could she even manage the unharnessing of the hobbled team and to lead them to Hartfordshire? If so, surely she'd meet Jackson on his return.

Nevertheless, indecision beleaguered her.

She'd attend to her personal needs then decide what to do.

Gingerly picking her way through the sparse underbrush, she at last found a well-concealed spot several yards from the road that promised more privacy. Yes, this would do nicely. Just to be on the safe side, she withdrew her dagger. One never knew what other creatures might seek a drink from the river this evening.

A short while later, having restored her knife to her boot and just as she lifted her skirts to step over a broad branch, far-off hoofbeats echoed. A relieved smile bent her mouth. Thank the Divine powers. She'd be home in time for dinner, after all, and a good long soak would take the chill from her bones.

And a toddy. Don't forget the toddy. Abundantly dosed with whisky.

Another luxury the Breckensoles rarely indulged in, but one enjoyed by the entire family on occasion.

A horseman called to the other, and upon hearing his rough Cockney-accented voice, she paused, one foot raised and head canted. These weren't riders from

Hartfordshire Court. Wisdom decreed she remain concealed until she learned exactly who they were. Hopefully, the smooth snake that had slithered across her path a few moments ago hadn't lingered.

With stealth and care, Gabriella retreated into the woods until the undergrowth grew denser once more. She crouched behind an ancient oak, her heart banging so fiercely against her breastbone, she feared the men would hear the loud staccato. Settling onto her knees, she flinched as the bruised flesh from being hurled onto the carriage floor objected. Making herself as small and inconspicuous as possible, she silently praised God that her green ensemble camouflaged her to a degree.

Breath held and squinting slightly, she peeked around the trunk, scrutinizing the travelers.

Upon spying the crippled coach, the two rough-looking men cantered to a stop. The portly older fellow slouched in his saddle, whilst a younger, thinner version of him considered the vehicle, a sly grin blooming across his grimy, unshaven face.

The hairs on her arms raised straight up from wrist

to shoulder, and she clapped a gloved hand over her mouth to keep from making any noise. *Oh, God.* Had they arrived a few minutes later, she would've already returned to the carriage. From their filthy, scruffy appearances, she'd be bound they weren't honorable sorts. Vagabonds, most likely.

"Well, well. Wot 'ave we 'ere, Wills?" Resting an elbow on his thick thigh, the older man leaned forward.

The younger chap chuckled and wiped his nose with the back of his hand. "An opportunity, Da."

As the men slid from their saddles, Gabriella shrank further to the root-ridden ground and closer to the trunk, scarcely daring to breathe. Fear's vice-like grip squeezed her lungs and cramped her burning throat.

Hitching up his baggy trousers, Wills opened the carriage door. He dangled one of Gabriella's packages in the doorway. "Looky 'ere."

Grandmama's medicine.

In short order, they tore her parcels open, tossing the chemises and Grandmama's remedies into the middle of the road. If that weren't awful enough, Wills stomped on the delicate undergarments before grinding the medicine bottles beneath his heel. The crunch of glass breaking sent a shudder through Gabriella and anger welling behind her ribs. *Damned rotter.* At least try to sell the items rather than destroy them.

He tipped the few coins remaining in her reticule into his grimy palm. The dainty bag, crocheted by Grandmama for Gabriella last Christmastide, met the same fate as the chemises. He crowed anew at discovering the pouch of tobacco and promptly stuffed it inside his coat.

The father held up the blue velvet cloak intended for Ophelia. "Wouldn't Miss Minnie like to prance 'round in dis?" He gave his son a lewd wink and minced around, swinging his large bum and the garment back and forth. "I'm bettin' she'd show 'er appreciation fer somfin' dis fancy." He grabbed his groin, imitating a vulgar movement.

"Do ye s'ppose she let me 'ave one of 'er fancier whores?" Wills bobbed his head and licked his lips. "One o' 'em gels tha' smell an' dresses pretty? And 'av nice teeth an' skin?"

"Not unless they've taken t' swivin' wif swine." His father hooted as he draped the cloak over his saddle. "Ye smell like a pig, son, an' rut like one too."

Sweat trickled a sticky path down her spine, and Gabriella swallowed against the burning nausea throttling up her throat. It was a good thing she hadn't eaten a midday meal, for it might very well have made a violent, noisy reappearance.

The frightened team neighed and pranced nervously, but Wills grabbed their harnesses, and cut the grays free.

They meant to steal Admiral and General. *God curse them. Fiends. Devil's spawns.*

Gabriella's stomach churned anew, and hot tears leaked from her eyes. Grandpapa had only purchased the pair last year, after waiting a lifetime to splurge on one of the few things he had ever wanted.

With gloating sneers curling their mouths, they mounted their horses and galloped away.

Wills's voice carried back to her. "I 'opes we come 'pon t' wench an' she's young. I 'aven't 'ad a good …"

Gabriella remained squatted in place for several long blinks. Her breathing ragged and uneven, she sluggishly stood upright using the coarse trunk to steady herself. If she hadn't sought privacy in the shrubberies, hadn't needed to relieve herself, she'd have been inside the carriage.

Wills would've…

Oh, God.

Another flash of icy-cold terror rippled over her.

No help for it now, she'd have to walk home and pray no more strangers ventured down the remote lane. Or that those two blackguards returned this way. She'd nearly reached the road when the unmistakable sound of another rider approaching met her ears.

Those hoofbeats also came from the direction of Colechester.

It had been months since she encountered another person on this isolated road, and today within minutes, she'd done so twice? Well, she hadn't actually *encountered* them because she concealed herself in the woods, but that was beside the point.

Retreating into the deepening shadows once more,

she awaited the horseman's approach with bated breath. Friend or foe? A means of sending word to home or another villain to avoid?

As had the other riders, the man—a gentleman from his expensively tailored attire—slowed his horse, and a low whistle preceded his, "Holy hell." Another muffled half-curse, half surprised exclamation escaped him as he stood in his stirrups surveying the conveyance. "What the blazes?"

Gabriella slid her eyelids shut and gave a short shake of her head. *No. No. It cannot be. Please, don't let it be.* Anyone…*anyone, dear God*...but *him*.

The Duke of Pennington was good and truly the last person she wanted to see right at this moment. Covered in dirt and leaves, tears dried upon her cheeks, and frightened half out of her mind she didn't have the strength to match wits with him. Not now. Not when her reserves were spent.

She raked her disbelieving gaze over his polished Hessians to track up his biscuit-colored buckskins stretched over muscled calves and thighs. He sat regal and self-confident. A man sure of himself and his position. She ventured higher still, past his buff-toned coat and brown leather-gloved hands gripping the reins, to his familiar granite jaw, the slashing blade of his nose, and his mismatched green and blue eyes beneath severe midnight eyebrows.

Blast, astride his mount he presented a fine figure of a man, her artist's discernment reluctantly conceded. How difficult would it be to capture the two distinct shades of his eyes on paper?

Just then, she swore he looked straight at her, directly through the greenery and the dusky twilight. Right into her eyes, as if he knew exactly where she stood, frozen in disbelief. A disconcerting jolt zipped to her stomach.

Dash it to ribbons.

Dash it to ribbons?

No, that didn't begin to describe her frustration. She blew a puff of air out her nose in a silent snort. Why did *he* of all people have to come along? After she'd pointedly told him to leave her alone.

The duke scrutinized the coach, then slowly, methodically inspected the surrounding area before his gaze came to rest on her hiding place once more.

He knows. He knew she hid here.

How?

That slow, lazy smile that so annoyed her she yearned to slap it from his handsome face, hitched his well-formed mouth skyward at the corners. He sank back into his saddle, casually looping his reins around one hand.

"Miss Breckensole, it's safe to come out now."

3

"*Merde*." Maxwell swore beneath his breath, examining the disabled coach once more. *What the hell happened here?* Obviously, the axel had snapped and the back wheel shattered, but why were these belongings strewn about? Another systematic sweep down the length of the road confirmed neither the coachman nor the team were anywhere to be seen.

Yet Gabriella was.

Had she opted to stay behind rather than ride one of the horses bareback to Hartsfordshire Court? Her driver ought to be sacked for leaving her here. What could the man have been thinking? No doubt, she had something to do with his absence, stubborn chit.

From beneath his eyelashes, he sliced a covert glance to the shadowy woods. Just .there, hovering half-concealed by that large tree, she still refused to come out of the forest. If she'd witnessed this destruction—and she most probably had—terror undoubtedly rendered her immobile.

If it hadn't been for her faint, involuntary gasp when he'd first reined Balor to a stop, he'd not have spied her either. All too familiar frustration and ire stiffened Max's shoulder muscles when he thought of Breckensole residing in the home that had once been in his paternal grandmother's family.

Not now. Soon, but not now.

Despite the sobriety of the moment, his lips twitched upward. She'd been outraged that he'd dared to ask her to go riding. He'd truly wanted her to accompany him on an outing, because despite everything, he liked her. Liked her very much, indeed. For months now, she'd fascinated him. Even before he'd learned of her grandfather's perfidy.

He could almost visualize the proper, but unpredictable, Gabriella Breckensole astride a horse in that green and black confection she'd been wearing in Colechester this afternoon. The image of her shapely legs exposed from ankle to thigh, hugging the horse's sides, created an unexpected but powerful sensual reaction. A response he'd have contemplated further if it weren't so bloody cold and darkness was quickly descending. Not that he was feeling particularly chilled. No, in fact inferior brandy yet warmed his gut.

However, if after her characteristically icy reception in Colechester, he hadn't indulged in two glasses at The Pony and Pint rather than his usual one, he'd have come upon the disabled vehicle sooner. And he might've been able to prevent this.

God's teeth. What if he'd gone beyond his usual restraints and quaffed the third brandy to help buffer the sharp abrasion of her scorn? Who knows what would've happened to her? As it was, even if he immediately took her before him on the saddle, they'd not make the house before night's mantle shrouded them.

What a remarkable idea, holding Gabriella Breckensole before him, his arms wrapped around her lush form, her rounded bum pressed into his thighs… *Egads, enough. She's likely frightened mute, and I'm indulging in lurid imaginations.* Besides, he did have a degree of pride. She'd all but snubbed him in Colechester and demanded he leave her alone. He couldn't though.

A slight movement caught his attention again. Nothing about her rigid, untrusting demeanor suggested she meant to join him on the road any time soon. Did she intend to continue lurking in the trees? All night? Was her loathing of him such she'd risk her safety or health by refusing to leave the concealment?

That knowledge grated, bitter and raw. When had she come to hate him? And more on point, why? He'd asked the question innumerable times. He did not, however, ask himself *why* he kept asking himself that question.

One hand braced on his hip, he swiped the back of the other across his forehead. By God, if the people who'd done this had known she was there… A vicious band tightened about his middle, stalling his breath for a long, gut-wrenching moment. He clenched his jaw against a wave of rage so powerful, the surge caused him pause.

They'd have set upon her. Harmed her. *Or worse*, damn the bloody bastards. Another swell of fury pelted his ribs. Was Gabriella injured? Blast him for a fool for not considering that straightaway. No woman should be subjected to something of this nature. It was ingrained in him to help, even if she didn't want his assistance. He'd do the same for anyone.

"Miss Breckensole?" When she remained silent, tension spiraled up his spine. The air left his lungs in a whoosh.

Christ above. Had she been…?

His eyelids flitted shut for an agonizing blink, and he set his jaw against the godawful thought he ought to have instantly considered. Mindful to keep the alarm from reaching his voice, he gently put forward, "Gabriella, are you…*unharmed*?"

Was there any other way to tactfully ask if she'd been set upon? Despoiled? Violated?

Only a sleepy bird's call punctuated the discomfiting silence.

"Yes. I'm fine." Her answer came as a faint whisper, so soft, he wasn't sure he'd heard her, yet she didn't move from the security of the woods.

Examining the horizon, he heaved a sigh then swung a leg over the saddle and hopped to the ground. "Do you intend to remain in the forest the entire night? There may well be all sorts of wild creatures—bears, wolves, badgers, lynx, and wolverines—hereabouts."

Perhaps not precisely *here*, but surely somewhere in the whole of England, hungry beasts roamed about stalking their next meal.

"Go bugger yourself, you pompous twit." Distinct vexation riddled the vixen's mutinous response.

He'd vow, she didn't think he'd heard her inappropriate comment.

Regardless of the seriousness of the situation, an unfettered chuckle escaped him. *Damn*, but he admired the minx's spirit. In fact, in his seven and twenty years, he'd never met a more extraordinary, frustrating woman. After tying Balor's reins to a nearby branch, Max shook his head in resignation, and with long strides, made directly for her.

Her harsh intake of breath earned her another derisive chuckle.

"Yes, I see you. You're most lucky the miscreants who destroyed your possessions did not." He jabbed a thumb in the sagging vehicle's direction. "I cannot leave you skulking in the greeneries, Miss Breckensole. Nightfall is nearly upon us, and though I confess, I cannot imagine why you are here and neither your coachman nor your team are present, a duke would never desert a lady in need."

"And of course, *you* always do what a duke would do, don't you?" she put forward, rapier sharp sarcasm dripping from each word.

Her accusation stung. As much from the utter contempt she hurled toward him as his lack of understanding why she felt such hostility. He bent into an exaggerated bow, made even more awkward given he straddled a log. Doffing his hat, he only just managing to keep from toppling face first into the dirt.

"Always, my dearest Miss Breckensole. Always."

Always, at least, when it came to her, damn his eyes. Which made the incredulous task he'd set himself equally pleasurable and disagreeable.

A theatrical sigh, followed by what most assuredly was another mumbled curse met his poetic declaration, and as he reached the road's edge, she emerged from her hiding place. Wariness lingered in the gaze she settled upon him. In the vanishing light, her hazel eyes appeared deep green, either a reflection from her gown or her verdant surroundings,

"Now, pray tell me," Max pointedly kept his tone light but empathetic as he gestured casually. "How, might I ask, came you to be here alone?"

"I am here, Your Grace, because as you can clearly see, my coach has a broken wheel and my driver, Jackson, went for help." She flung a gloved hand, the palm dirt-smeared, toward the abused vehicle.

Your coach has a great deal more wrong with it than a broken wheel. Rather than state the obvious, he asked, "How long have you been stranded?"

Frowning down at the timepiece pinned to her spencer, she crinkled her nose adorably.

Were those new freckles atop the bridge? He

hadn't noticed them earlier today.

"My coachman left over two hours ago." Pert chin jutted forward and ignoring the hand he extended to assist her onto the road, she swept past him as regally as any of Almacks' elegant patronesses. "I cannot imagine what's keeping Jackson." As she stood in the middle of the road, her arms folded, she gave the slightest, befuddled shake of her head.

A bit of moss drifted to the ground.

Gabriella tracked the movement with her keen-eyed gaze. Her mouth pulled into a prim line before she anchored those arresting, thick-lashed eyes on him with a don't-you-dare-laugh look. Shaking out her skirts, little bits of twigs, leaves, and dirt spilling around her feet, she searched the road again and a bit of tension left her. She relaxed her stiff shoulders and lowered her chin.

Even rumpled, frazzled, her hem soiled, and dirt clinging to her gown, in the fading light she was a radiant jewel. A forest nymph: mysterious and untamed and utterly bewitching.

She squatted and gingerly lifted the shredded

remnant of what appeared to be a night shift or perhaps a chemise. A perplexed frowned wrinkled her brow as she spread both hands wide, staring at the destruction. "I don't understand…*this*. Why would anyone do this? Be so despicable? So destructive for no reason? Such vileness is beyond me."

Dropping the mangled cloth, she swallowed audibly, and compassion swelled within his chest. *The darling, brave girl.* Were those dried tears on her face? Impossible to tell in the half-light, but a definite dirt smudge slashed across one porcelain cheek. He'd dipped his hand halfway to his coat pocket to fetch his handkerchief to wipe her face before he stopped himself. Not only didn't he have the right, these tender sentiments toward her muddled his determination.

Nonetheless, he admired her gumption. She was much more affected than she let on. But then, what woman wouldn't be?

If he took her in his arms and comforted her as he ached to do, she'd likely box his ears or punch him in the nose. Or both. She'd probably stomp his foot and elbow his ribs too. He'd not mind all that much if doing so removed the haunted look from her arresting eyes.

Max extended a hand again, and this time, after a long, long moment's hesitation where he was certain she meant to refuse his offer of assistance once more, she slid her fingers into his palm. He helped her stand upright. "What the devil happened, Miss Breckensole?"

"You can see what they did for yourself, Your Grace." She promptly withdrew her hand then wiped it on her skirt.

He scowled. Was his touch so unwelcome? "Tell me anyway."

She released a fragile little laugh, spreading both hands wide once more. "Two ruffians came along. They also stole Ophelia's birthday present and the team." Her bravado slipped a notch, and her lower lip trembled the merest bit before she ticked that stubborn chin upward once more. "Grandpapa will be devastated."

Probably because the miser would have to purchase another team. Did the skinflint's coffers creak and groan from infrequent use when he was forced to lift the lid to extract money?

Everyone far and wide knew Harold Breckensole for an uncharitable tightwad. A man who never paid the asking price for anything and a pinchfist misanthrope who rarely gave so much as a groat to those less fortunate. He was also the unconscionable bounder who'd swindled Max's grandfather and purchased Hartfordshire Court and the surrounding five-and-forty acres for a bloody pittance.

He cheated and blackmailed Grandfather.

Max shook loose his morose meanderings. This wasn't the time, but he had a plan, and by God, old Breckensole would pay dearly for his shady dealings. Indeed, the bloody blighter would. And soon. Very soon.

Two fingers pressed to his temple, Max studied the ruined garments and torn wrapping papers scattered about the ground. This act bespoke hatred and vengeance. "Your coachman's been gone for upward of two hours, you say?" More than enough time to walk to Hartfordshire Court and return.

Gabriella responded with a single, terse nod.

She'd behaved this way since this past December. Since that Christmas house-party they'd attended as guests of the Duke and Duchess of Sutcliffe. One day, she'd been warm and welcoming, her sable-fringed hazel eyes sparkling and her kissable petal-pink lips smiling. The next morning, a warrior's practiced scowl upon those same lovely features and thunder darkening her eyes to steely gray, she'd become brusque and cold, avoiding him as if he were covered in oozing sores.

Which made the task he'd set himself—to woo and marry her to gain Hartfordshire Court once more—all the more difficult. He well knew Breckensole's only heirs were the twins. Yes, Max's man of business had done his research. He also knew Breckensole's dirty little secret. A secret he'd most certainly wouldn't want his granddaughters to learn.

Worried Gabriella would think his rage was directed toward her, he lowered his eyelids against the fury he feared glinted there and unrelentingly twisted his gut.

Of its own accord, his attention swept her shapely figure. Mayhap this incident might be used in his favor. She required rescuing, though he hadn't a single doubt she'd deny it with her last breath. And Providence had seen to it that he came along at an opportune moment where she was hard-put to toss his chivalry back in his face.

He rather liked playing the gallant for her.

True, a smidgeon of remorse for what he intended to do poked its unwanted head up. But Max reconciled his guilt with the knowledge she and her sister would be well-cared for after Breckensole's ruination.

His ire wasn't directed at the twins, or even the old man's wife, for that matter. No, the sole recipient of Max's disgust and retribution was Harold Breckensole; the man directly or indirectly responsible for the deaths of four of Max's family members.

His regard sank to Gabriella's tapping toes. *Left foot. Right foot. Left foot. Right foot.* A cadence of annoyance clearly revealing her impatience. Did she know she drummed her feet whenever aggravated? He checked a smile. She was so easy to read. He'd wager at this very moment, she skewed her mouth back and forth in a winsome fashion, something else she did whenever vexed or anxious. A fashion that made him very much want to kiss those lush lips she'd nibbled to a raspberry red in her frustration.

"Do you think the constable will be able to find Grandpapa's horses?" she asked. After all she'd been through, her concern was for her grandfather.

He wouldn't lift a finger to help Breckensole, but he would for her. "Quite possibly. The team is unusual and not easily forgotten. I can put the word out to sources I know to have them stay on alert."

Her expression contemplative, she continued to torture the soil with her toes.

Given the dainty, thin-soled slippers she wore, he wasn't at all surprised she hadn't walked home as well. Her tramp into the forest had undoubtedly ruined the footwear though. "Most wise of you to conceal yourself in the woodlands until your man returned."

A surprised, discomfited look flitted across her pale features, which she concealed almost instantly. Not meeting his gaze, she cleared her throat.

"*Erm*…yes. Exactly so."

Even in the faint light he didn't miss the rosy hue sweeping across her cheeks as she became suddenly fixated on the trees' silhouettes. *Ah.* His mind had stumbled upon the awkward truth, and to spare her further embarrassment, he cupped her elbow. "Come, let's be away from here. I cannot help but feel it's not altogether safe for us to remain."

She trained her gaze on the wreckage and put a slightly unsteady hand to her forehead. Was she hurt worse than she let on? Or did emotion overwhelm her?

He squinted one eye, and for the first time noticed the ugly discoloration on her forehead. "Miss Breckensole, you *are* injured."

Bending slightly nearer, he lifted the edge of her bonnet. Intoxicating and seductive, her perfume wafted upward. Nostrils flared, he breathed in her essence: lavender and something lemony? Mayhap a hint of jasmine as well.

The heady combination sent Max's senses reeling, and it took all of his restraint to keep from nuzzling the slim, ivory column of her throat where the fragrance surely lingered on her satiny skin. Annoyance pelted him. He needed to wrestle his attraction to her under control. She was a means to an end. She couldn't be anything more.

Before I found my grandfather's journal, she could've been.

He'd very much wished her to be.

"You didn't answer. Are you hurt?" He skimmed her from head to toe. She hadn't limped as she exited the woods, and he detected no obvious abrasions.

"Not seriously." She tilted her head, her eyes round with uncertainty. "A slight bump on my head and sore knees. I'm far more worried about my grandfather's reaction to all of this. Grandmama's too. She's not been well."

He'd known that before she made mention of it in the village today. Truthfully, there wasn't much he didn't know about the Breckensoles. He'd made it his business. *Know one's enemy,* Father had drilled into him as had his father before him. And *his* before him.

Head cocked, he combed his gaze over her refined features. White lines of strain bracketed her mouth and crimped the corners of her lovely eyes. Reaching into his coat pocket, he retrieved a flask. After twisting the cap off, he offered the silver casket to her.

A delicate, tawny eyebrow lifted mockingly.

She probably had no idea what the contents were. In general, gentle-bred young ladies didn't go about quaffing strong spirits. Still, a bottle of the stuff was delivered to Hartfordshire Court monthly, so someone imbibed, albeit not heavily.

"It's whisky," he offered by way of explanation, levering the flask up and down.

And as Miss Gabriella Breckensole had done on almost every occasion he'd encountered her, she'd flummoxed him once again. "I am not so very ignorant, Your Grace. I know what it is."

A wry smile tipping her soft oh-so-kissable lips, she accepted the flask and wrapping that rosebud mouth around the opening, took a hearty swallow. Not a dainty, feminine sip. No indeed. She took a gulp worthy of any healthy young buck and didn't cough and gasp afterward as many a gent was wont to do.

Max could almost feel the sharp sting on his

tongue and the fiery trail burning to his stomach. A craving to taste the spirit on her mouth, to tease the flavor from her tongue, slammed into him, obliterating his rationale for what he planned to do to her.

4

That stunning hunger, unequal and startling in its potency, set Max back on his heels.

Control. Yourself. He thundered silently. *She's the means to an end. Nothing more. She cannot be.*

He really had become a selfish bastard, all in the name of vengeance for a sin committed decades before he'd been born. Yes, but he'd seen the effects played out and now understood his Grandfather's choosing to drink himself into oblivion rather than face a single day sober.

Eyes closed, Gabriella took another swig and gave a delicate shudder. She swallowed and thrust her arm straight out. "Here. I've had enough, thank you."

"Are you *quite* certain?" Max couldn't prevent the

humor filtering into his voice as he topped the case before tucking it back into his pocket.

"Yes. Quite." A heated glower accompanied her pithy retort.

There was the spirited vixen he'd come to expect. The one that had told him to go bugger himself. The one who lifted her nose and thrust her mutinous, dimpled chin upward whenever their gazes clashed. The one who snubbed and cut him at every opportunity.

And yet, his captivation waned not a jot. If anything, her allure grew. Considering his animosity toward her grandfather, and hers toward Max, did that make him perverse? Or mad? Or both, mayhap?

None of that mattered. Achieving his goal was the only thing—*the only thing*—that did.

He untied his horse's reins. "As I cannot in good conscience leave you here to await your coachman's return, Miss Breckensole, you'll have to ride before me on Balor."

Before she could object, he grasped her narrow waist, his hands almost spanning the circumference, and lifted her onto the horse's back, both of her svelte legs dangling over the near side.

Through his gloves, his palms burned from the intimate contact. He might've let his hands linger an instant longer than was completely necessary. Too bad he couldn't encourage her to ride astride. On second thought, that was a bloody awful notion. He'd explode in his pantaloons if he had to watch those creamy thighs flex and ripple as they gripped Balor.

Giving him a fuming glare, she clutched Balor's mane, and before she could slip to the ground, Max leapt into the saddle behind her. Securing her firmly around her slim waist, he lowered his mouth near her ear.

"Don't be foolish, Gabriella. We have but the one horse, and you're wearing slippers. I shall not leave you here to await your coachman. The miscreants who stole your team could very well return." Not likely, but not impossible either. "As much as you dislike me, I am a gentleman, and I shall see you safely home."

She grunted her displeasure and jerked away, in the process bumping his already sensitized groin. He stifled a groan. It was going to prove to be one bloody uncomfortable ride.

Bowing her head in what he could only assume was resignation, she muttered, "I haven't given you leave to use my Christian name, and neither am I fool enough to throw myself from a horse, Your Grace."

"I don't believe you a fool at all, *chérie*."

She stiffened before elbowing him hard in the stomach.

"Oomph," he grunted, not daring to rub the offended flesh, else she slip loose, but he took the opportunity to lurch forward and brush his lips across one dainty ear. *Tit for tat, chérie.*

"I am not now, nor will I ever be *your* sweetheart, you buffoon," she finished rather breathlessly.

We shall see, sweet Gabriella. We shall see.

A stupid grin slashed Max's mouth upward. He'd felt the tremor running through her, recognized the subtle shudder for what it was. Desire. For all of Miss Gabriella Breckensole's protestations of dislike for him, her young body said something much, much different. And he could, and would, use that to his advantage.

Inordinately pleased by the discovery, with a click of his tongue and a nudge to Balor's sides, he directed his sturdy black toward Hartfordshire Court. "Walk on."

Stick straight and just as inflexible, Gabriella rode before him, doing her utmost to keep her behind—any part of her body for that matter—from brushing his.

"Miss Breckensole, you can relax against me. Upon my word, I promise to act the perfect gentleman."

A distinctly unladylike snort met his declaration. "And I'm the Queen of Sheba."

He'd much prefer to address her as Gabriella or *chérie*, enjoying the way the syllables rolled off his tongue, but he wouldn't put it past her to leap to the ground just to prove her point.

Chin tucked, he glowered at the bonnet hiding her luxurious, rich honey-brown hair threaded with golden ribbons from his appreciative gaze. He gave her waist a little prod, and she jumped, rearing her head back and smacking him solidly in the jaw.

That would bruise, he'd be bound.

"It's two miles to Hartfordshire." He nudged her once more. "Relax."

She acted as if she'd sooner ride bald and bare-ass-naked through Hyde Park than allow any part of her body to touch him. Her rejection shouldn't rankle, but it did. And while Max didn't consider himself a rapscallion per se, he wasn't a stranger to the joys of a woman's form or the pleasures that could be found with a willing bed partner.

He'd also evaded his fair share of huntresses in full cry, their title-hungry mamas, directing their eager daughter's every move as they tried to snare a duke. Tried to trap him, to be exact. There hadn't been a ball, soiree, assembly, picnic, or rout that he hadn't been eyed like a prize stallion by debutantes, spinsters, wallflowers, heiresses, and the occasional widow too.

He held no illusions of marital bliss. His parents' union had been less than idyllic.

Of their own volition, his lips kicked up into a sardonic smirk.

But Max's grandfather had adored his

grandmother. So much so that after she died, he'd moved the household to London and refused to stay at Chartworth Hall. Grandfather had been an empty shell of a man, given to too much drink, going days on end without bathing or dressing. And in the end, he took his own life, because he couldn't bear living without his beloved wife.

If that was love, Max could well do without the castrating emotion.

It was his turn to snort, and Gabriella sent him a puzzled, sideways look.

Nevertheless, her aversion to him exasperated. He was the highly sought-after Duke of Pennington. Known for his wit and jovial temperament. His vices were few: a fine cognac or whisky, the occasional cheroot, and superior horseflesh. He didn't keep a mistress—not for the lack of offers—and he was honest and fair; judiciously so most of the time.

And yet, the minx grudgingly riding before him couldn't abide him. Mayhap that was why he found her so intriguing. No, if he were honest with himself, he'd found her remarkable, *too remarkable*, before she'd turned her icy disdain upon him. He gave a slight shake of his head, reining in his wayward musings. It mattered not.

She would be his bride and the dowry he'd insist upon was Hartfordshire Court. Nothing else would do. He had no compunction about resorting to extreme measures. His own version of blackmail, if need be. Nothing and no one kept him from something once he'd set his mind to it.

Her grandfather was responsible for Max's grandmother's and grandfather's deaths. Even Father's, though he conceded, that was a bit of a stretch. His father's tendency to drink and gamble to excess, as well as his less than discriminating taste in the women he took to bed had been his downfall. He'd tried to hire a strumpet already engaged with a ship's captain. There'd been a fight and the captain had stabbed the seventh duke in the stomach. The wound had grown putrid, the infection spread, and he'd died a horrifying death.

Breckensole *would* pay.

Gabriella made a little noise—likely involuntary.

No doubt her thoughts also tumbled about in her head. Her parents were dead as well. He wracked his brain, trying to remember how old the twins were when they came to live with their grandparents. He'd been at Eton by then.

Recalling her puckered expression at the Christmastide dinner before she swiftly assumed the bland mien she presented to him when she'd found herself seated beside him, a silent chuckle shook his chest. Their hostess, the Duchess of Sutcliffe, might have served vermin in white sauce for all the attention Gabriella had paid to the food that evening. Her ability to answer his questions with clipped one-word responses and to resolutely direct her attention to her other dinner partner surely had to be a feat worthy of recognition.

Why, he supposed he ought to be flattered she'd actually strung more than two words together in conversation with him in the village and since he'd come upon her this afternoon.

Given Max was hell-bent on having her home returned to his family, he had no business—*none whatsoever*—entertaining this perverse interest in her. And yet the more she resisted him, the more she disdained his presence, ignored the tipping of his hat or the extending of his elbow, the more captivated he became. That either made him dicked in the nob, or…

By God, he wasn't sure what that made him.

Stupid? Imbecilic? Pathetic? *A predator?*

That disagreeable thought stuck fast in his craw, mostly due to the degree of truth in the ugly acknowledgement. It gave him a sour taste in his mouth. Nonetheless, he must remain rational at all costs. He couldn't afford to let his emotions become entangled even if she was to become his duchess and the mother of his heir and spare. He'd permit his lust for her free rein, but never anything more.

As much to catch another whiff of her unique perfume as to spare her the sore muscles she would endure tomorrow if she continued holding her unnatural posture, he leaned into her slender back, and pressing one palm into her middle urged her against him. "I said relax," he breathed into her ear.

"Are you always such an arrogant bully?" Even as

she muttered the words, a ragged almost wistful sigh juddered her shoulders, and she sank into his chest.

Most women of his acquaintance would've dissolved into histrionics or tears had they been forced to huddle in the forest and witness their possessions destroyed and horses stolen. Not to mention deigning to relieve themselves in those same woods. Not Miss Gabriella Breckensole. She refused to show weakness to anyone.

That was one of the things he most admired about her. Her stubbornness. Her independence. Her I-don't-need-your-help-I-can-do-it-myself bravado. The almost intractable child-like attitude that lit a spark in her eyes and bent her lips into an endearing, mulish slant. It was also what would make his task more difficult.

In the beginning, she might resent their marriage, but with her keen wit and intellect, she'd make an extraordinary duchess. He was confident of the fact. Their desire was mutual, and that was nothing to scoff at. Even if they never claimed the love his grandparents had.

After stumbling upon his grandfather's journal in the study a few months ago, Max had sworn an oath to avenge him. He'd replaced the ancient, scarred monstrosity of a desk with a smaller one. Whilst the four hirelings labored to lift the old piece, a hidden drawer had popped open, revealing the leather-bound book.

The first entry that had leapt out at him—had burned in his mind since.

August 1744

I told Margaret that Hartfordshire Court was sold. How she sobbed when I confessed I'd been forced to sell her childhood home to Harold Breckensole.

The rotter blackmailed me into selling it. He'd vowed he'd have his revenge on me, because he fancied a little tart who climbed into my bed, and now he has. The lying bastard claims he caught me cheating at cards. The bloody sot even went so far as to enlist those insolent pups up from university, Wakefield and Garrison, to act as witnesses. Those two bounders will do anything for a drink, a whore, and a few pounds.

The cards were marked, but not by me. Breckensole must have marked them and then framed me. I cannot prove it, and when he threatened to make the disgrace public, I feared what the scandal and shunning would do to Margaret. Feared she'd quicken early again. And so, in desperation, I agreed to his damnable terms. I couldn't risk her miscarrying yet another heir.

My heir must come before all else. He must. The ducal lineage must continue.

Breckensole's bloody terms included a legal bill of sale and a contract between us that no one could ever know about the marked cards. He thinks he's been so clever. He's the victor for now, but someday, his scheme will come back to bite him in the arse. I've made sure of it.

I only agreed to his extortion for my heir's sake. Margaret's losing three babes in as many years has made me a mad man. Her health is frail and grows more so. She weeps incessantly. That is enough to drive me madder still. I should have married a woman with a stronger constitution, but how does any man know his wife's womb will fail?

While Margaret was with child, she couldn't know I'd sold Hartfordshire Court, so I waited six months until I was sure our son would live.

At long last I have my heir.

Only a few short, terse entries followed, two of which stuck in Max's mind:

Reverend Michael Shaw was killed in a duel.

Egads, what could a reverend have done to find himself challenged to an affair of honor? Preached on adultery? Bigamy? Helped himself to the tithes?

The last entry sent a queer chill up his spine.

Margaret is dead. She was with child.

And Breckensole was to blame, damn his covetous soul to hell. Well, not the particular entry about the reverend, but the rest could be laid at his feet.

The hushed whisper he'd heard once as a child that his grandmother had flung herself down the stairs had been nothing more than gossip from the lower orders, his father had insisted. His own mother had died within two years of giving birth to him, and he had no memory of her except for woeful, nondescript brown eyes in a plump, plain face.

From beneath half-closed eyelids, Max considered Gabriella. Her slim nape and sloping shoulders, the dip of her slender waist and her hips that flared out into luscious curves. Curves he itched to run his hands over.

Yes, she was far better than the simpering misses he was accustomed to having hanging on his arm, batting their eyelashes, and incapable of stringing an intelligent sentence together let alone retrieving their own handkerchief or fan from the floor.

He'd rip his hair out by the roots and run screaming from the room if forced to endure another inane conversation about the weather, who was seen riding with whom in Hyde Park, or the latest *on dit* in the gossip rags.

Only their breathing and the rhythmic *clip-clopping* of Balor's hooves punctuating the peaceful evening stillness, Max and Gabriella rode for several minutes. Unfortunately, no moon illuminated their way, although an occasional brave star peeked from amongst the cloud-ridden sky.

He wasn't concerned, however. Many were the times he'd traveled this road with the heavens darker than this. His estate lay little more than a half mile beyond Hartfordshire Court. Even decades after that bounder Breckensole had cheated Max's grandfather of the manor and grounds, he refused to refer to the estate as Breckensole's.

"Gabriella?" he put forth, even as his instinct warned him to stop.

"Hmm?" she murmured sleepily as she half-turned her head to look into his eyes. Sloe-eyed, her face softened by fatigue and her guard down, her earlier hostility had disappeared and something indefinable held him in thrall.

Another peculiar tightening contracted his ribs.

Why did she of all women have to affect him thusly? The granddaughter of his grandfather's nemesis and by extension, his as well?

He couldn't see her expression clearly in the inky blackness, and his usual confidence wobbled for a moment. Grazing his knuckles along her silky jaw, he asked softly, “What have I done to offend you?”

5

Darkness hid the blush blooming across Gabriella's face at the duke's intimate touch upon her skin. For God help her, the harsh retort hovering on the tip of her tongue evaporated, and—*how could it possibly be?* —she yearned to press her cheek into his gloved hand.

She blamed fear, hunger, and worry about her grandfather's reaction. *Yes, of course, that's it.* Her anxiety and fretting caused her to harbor such uncharacteristic, fanciful notions. Certainly not a desire to have the duke caress her.

But how should she answer his question?

It would be pure foolishness to make him aware

she knew about his dastardly scheme to reclaim Hartfordshire Court. Fine, mayhap she didn't *precisely* know what that plot was or how the duke planned to enact it, but she did know he intended to do that very thing.

"Help. Help."

The weak cry saved her from having to answer the duke's prying query. Straightening, straining her eyes, she made out the shadowy rocky contours of the arched stone bridge.

"Help me, please. I'm down here, on the embankment."

As the plea echoed through the darkness once more, the duke slowed his powerful horse. His muscular body taut, Pennington brushed against Gabriella's back as he pulled upright.

"Jackson," she breathed, clutching the duke's forearm and twisting to catch his gaze. Or at least she tried to. In the dim light, she could only make out the edges of his hewn features. "That's my coachman. I know his voice. He must be hurt."

That was why he hadn't returned.

With a short nod—at least she thought the duke nodded. The darkness made it so very difficult to tell—he said, "Stay here. I'll check on his condition."

As soon as he slipped from the saddle and ventured down the embankment, she rolled onto her stomach and slid from the horse as well. She hurried over to the bridge, and one hand holding the rough, rocky edge, leaned over. Only obscure shadowy shapes met her scrutiny. *Curses.* Why couldn't there have been a moon tonight? They hadn't even the convenience of the coach lamp to light the area.

"Jackson, it's Miss Gabriella. Are you hurt?"

A sharp oath met her ears. "Miss Breckensole, I told you to remain on my horse." Flint-like annoyance accented each short syllable the duke rasped.

Yes, he had, and she'd chosen to disregard his directive. He might be accustomed to having his every wish promptly granted, but he wasted his breath ordering her about.

"Your Grace, as I am not your servant, hireling or wife, I don't feel obliged to obey your commands. Most particularly when Jackson is a member of *my* household." Her words rang every bit as pompous and harsh in the quiet of the night, and immediate chagrin for her churlishness sluiced her. She refused to become a harpy, even if he did vex her to next December and beyond.

The duke had been nothing but kind, helpful, and gentlemanly.

She could almost like this considerate man. If only… *If only.* If wishes were horses, beggars would ride, as Grandpapa was wont to quote.

"Jackson, are you badly hurt?" she called, regret softening her voice.

A loud, pain-filled groan met her question. "I fear my leg's broken, miss."

She sucked in an abrupt breath. If the duke hadn't come along when he had… Hanging farther over the bridge's side, she squinted at the two indistinguishable men below. "However did you end up down there?"

"I only meant to have myself a drink of water, but the ground gave way, and I tumbled," Jackson answered. "I'm sorry, Miss Breckensole."

"You've nothing to be sorry for," Gabriella

assured him.

However, Grandpapa would chew nails at another unexpected expense, for the servants' care fell to him. A new, most unpleasant, thought struck her. Her grandparents and Ophelia would be frantic that she hadn't returned from Colechester yet. Even as the truth crossed her mind, the rumble of an approaching conveyance rent the night air, overwhelming the crickets' chirps and frogs' croaking.

There, across the old arced bridge, a conveyance came from Hartfordshire's direction. Either Grandpapa or the young groom. No one else knew how to tool a vehicle. She'd asked to learn but had been denied the privilege.

"Someone's coming." She turned, waving her arms up and down in the unlikely event the driver didn't see her.

One arm around Jackson's waist and the other holding the servant's arm across Max's broad shoulders, the men labored up the incline. The carriage lamps sent an eerie glow over the road as the landau drew to an uneven stop.

"Gabriella girl, is that you?" Grandpapa squinted into the night. "Where are the coach and team?"

"Yes, Grandpapa, it's me. I'm afraid the coach lost a wheel, and Jackson's hurt." Best not to tell him the condition of the coach or that his team had been stolen just yet. As an afterthought she added, "The Duke of Pennington is here as well. He came to our aid."

She sensed as much as saw her grandfather go rigid and defensive.

"We don't need or accept help from a Woolbright or any Duke of Pennington," Grandpapa all but growled in a gravelly tone she'd never heard from him before.

The air fairly crackled with enmity, and her jaw hung slack. Never before had she witnessed such hostility from her gentle, eccentric grandfather. Was it possible he was already aware of the duke's plans to try to force them from their home? That certainly would warrant well-earned antagonism. God knew it had caused hers.

To Pennington's credit, he didn't respond in kind

but continued to assist the injured coachman to the waiting carriage. That raised him a notch in her estimation—to worm rather than maggot.

"Can you step into the conveyance?" Pennington asked Jackson, covered with muck and grass streaks. "I'll bear your weight and balance you."

She'd never known a peer to expend effort for a commoner, let alone soil his fancy—*expensive*—clothing or muddy his fine—*very expensive*—boots.

"Aye, Your Grace." Muttering a muffled oath, Jackson braced his arms on the open door then giving a tremendous heave, levered himself onto the cushion. With a low groan, he collapsed into the corner, and even in the half-light, Gabriella recognized the strain creasing his pale face.

"Gabriella, take a seat at once," Grandpapa all but snapped, including her in his curmudgeon's glare. "Your grandmother and sister are beside themselves with worry, and I must retrieve the team as soon as I've seen you home."

Oh no. How can I tell Grandpapa?

She raised what surely must be stricken eyes to the

duke's. Why she'd look to him for help or reassurance she couldn't begin to speculate. Simply put, it seemed the most natural thing in the world to do.

Something akin to compassion transformed the granite-like angled planes of Pennington's face. His strong mouth softened and tipped up at the corners. "Breckensole, I regret your team's been stolen and your coach has a broken axel." Sympathy rather than gloating tempered Pennington's somber tone. "I came upon the wreckage and found your granddaughter huddled in the woods, terrified for her life."

Eyelids sliding closed, Gabriella gave a whimpering groan. *Bother and blast.* She believed she'd been so stoic and brave—had hidden her fear so well.

"What…? What say you?" Grandpapa brought his aghast gaze up to swing between her and Pennington. He whispered brokenly, "My…my team stolen? My coach destroyed?" His stooped shoulders slumped, and he hung his head.

Gabriella tried to reach up to pat his arm. "I'm so sorry, Grandpapa. Maybe if I'd stayed in the coach…"

She'd have been despoiled, for certain.

"No, Miss Breckensole. You were wise to hide." In an instant, flint-like censure turned Pennington's speech ruthless and unforgiving. "I should think you'd be more concerned with your granddaughter's wellbeing, Breckensole. A coach and team are replaceable. Something as precious as her cannot ever be."

An odd inflection roughened his last words.

She caught his eye and gave a small shake of her head. He'd only make things worse, pointing out the obvious truth to her grandfather. She was still trying to come to terms with the loss herself. It was easier for a man as wealthy as the duke to consider acquiring a new matched pair and commissioning another coach a minor inconvenience. Not as true for her family.

Her grandfather's head snapped up, and she almost gasped at the loathing contorting his lined face. "How dare you imply I don't care for my granddaughter?"

What had happened to cause such visceral enmity between him and the Dukes of Pennington? He'd been remarkably closed-mouthed about it all these years, whatever it was. He'd known the twins encountered the duke at social events and never hinted they were to avoid him.

Had something occurred of late to change that?

But what?

A growing suspicion niggled, and though she couldn't put her finger on just what made her uneasy, Gabriella was convinced Grandpapa kept something significant from her, Grandmama, and Ophelia.

"Just like an arrogant Pennington, passing judgment on others." Grandpapa's mouth twisted into a contemptuous sneer. "Always thinking you're superior to everyone else, whilst forgetting the plank in your own eyes."

"At least we're honest and forthright in our business and *other* dealings." Gone was the tender duke who'd cradled her in his preposterously strong arms as they sat atop his horse. This man glaring daggers at her feeble grandfather she could very well believe would put them from their home without a qualm.

"Just exactly what are you implying, Pennington?" Grandpapa asked slowly, his rancor palpable in the set of his shoulders and the muscle flexing in his jaw. He raised his crop threateningly, and for a blink, Gabriella feared he meant to strike Pennington.

She rushed to intervene. Striking a peer, let alone a duke, would have harsh consequences. "Grandpapa, after the axel broke, ruffians came along. They stole the team and the mazurine velvet cloak I commissioned for Ophelia's birthday present." His tobacco too, but she'd spare him that triviality. "They also stomped upon Grandmama's medicines and destroyed our new chemises."

"Why?" Sorrow and disbelief riddled the clipped word. "I've made no enemies."

Save the Penningtons, it would seem. Neither had he made friends, and that knowledge saddened her.

The night had grown brisk, and a frigid shudder stole down her spine. Shivering, she rubbed her arms in a vain attempt to warm herself. "I don't know why," she admitted in a hushed tone.

He swung an accusing gaze at the duke. "I'll be

bound it was no mere coincidence. No, by God, this smacks of Pennington deviousness."

"Grandpapa!" Pennington might mean to reclaim his familial home, but until today, there'd not been a single instance of nefarious behavior. Nothing suspicious directed at the Breckensoles. "If the duke hadn't come upon Jackson and me and lent us his assistance, we'd both be stranded right now."

Well, she wouldn't have been, because she'd have walked home.

Her defense of the duke earned her a furious glare from her grandfather and an enigmatic half-smile from the man himself. Unexpected pleasure burgeoned behind her ribs. The duke was pleased she'd defended him. How absurd, and how unlike her. Still, she wasn't so churlish as to refuse to give credit where it was due. They did owe him a debt of gratitude.

"I'll ride to Colechester to fetch the doctor," Pennington offered after handing Gabriella into the carriage.

His touch burned through her gloves, and continued to heat her palm after she'd claimed a spot on the seat.

Pale and drawn, his injured leg thrust out before him, Jackson rested his head upon the squab.

Grandpapa gave the duke a dark scowl. "I already told you, we don't need help from the likes of you."

Pennington closed the door and dipped his head. He'd unfastened his coat and lost his hat. A shock of raven hair hung boyishly over his brow. She'd never seen him other than immaculately groomed and found his partial dishabille rather appealing. It made him less intimidating. More her equal. Which, of course, he was not.

There was a lot about the Duke of Pennington she found appealing—or had found appealing before she discovered the fine trappings and impeccable manners hid a completely different man. An unethical sod bent on her family's destruction. That knowledge filled her with an aching sadness, caused by more than disappointment.

There was no denying the secret thrill that had zipped from her hips to shoulders as his solid muscled thighs bunched against her bum or the welcoming hard-planed wall of his chest she'd sagged into as she rode before him. What woman wouldn't find such blatant maleness tempting?

Dangerous musings I'd best put an end to at once.

Any benevolent thoughts toward the Duke of Pennington were misplaced. He meant to put them out of their home. *Don't forget that,* no matter how solicitous and pleasant he might be at this moment.

Besides, something dark, intense, and secret simmered between him and her grandfather. And it was powerful and eerie enough to make her nape tingle. It also stirred her curiosity, and she meant to find out what it was. Instinct told her it had something to do with the duke's plan to claim Hartfordshire Court.

With a concerned glance toward Jackson, Gabriella said, "Grandpapa, please be reasonable. We do need Pennington's help. None of us is capable of driving into town tonight, and if Jackson's leg is truly broken, he cannot wait until tomorrow to have it set." She scooted to the edge of the seat mindful of her grandfather's mulish silence. "Your Grace, we'd be most grateful for your assistance."

"Always a pleasure, Miss Breckensole." From his genial low-timbred tone, she could almost believe he meant it.

One hand on the vehicle's side, she said softly, "Thank you…for everything."

Giving his head the merest inclination, his mouth slid upward a jot, but it was a far cry from a sincere smile. "You never answered my question," he murmured for her ears alone, giving the tips of her fingers a little squeeze.

What have I done to offend you?

His probing, confused gaze made the inquiry again, and if she didn't know better, if the shadows weren't playing with her senses, she might've detected the merest thread of hurt. Surely, he didn't expect her to answer now? Especially here? Particularly when Grandpapa looked as if he'd like to take the crop to him, duke or not?

Her movement barely discernable, she shifted her head and eyes to indicate she wouldn't answer. She hadn't a doubt he'd ask her again, and she was sorely tempted to tell him the truth of it just to see what he'd say.

Would he lie, deny it, or make an excuse? Or would he own his words and explain himself? She so wanted it to be the latter, no matter how irrational. Disgust at her traitorous inclinations brought her up short, retangling the confused knot in her empty belly.

Maxwell, the frustratingly attractive and enigmatic Duke of Pennington was the enemy. Was *her* enemy. She'd be an utter fool to believe any of the smooth words he put forth. Wasn't that what the serpent in the Garden of Eden had done? Used his wiles to trick and deceive Eve?

But… would a man bent on causing harm to her family have been so helpful? Or, what if his assistance had all been a guise to win them over? To put her off the scent? Her musings circled around and around like a dog chasing its tail.

Bah. She was too tired, cold, and hungry to cobble more than two coherent thoughts together. Besides, Pennington wasn't aware she was onto his game. That gave her an advantage, albeit only a slight one, but one she meant full well to use.

With another polite angling of his dark head and a ghost of a bow, the duke presented his back, and a moment later, leapt into the saddle and rode away.

As improbable, illogical, and yes, utterly ridiculous as it was, an odd bereftness encompassed Gabriella. *Fool. Ninny. Goose cap.* She loathed the man. Despised him for what he intended to do to Grandpapa. To all of the Breckensoles.

But she'd spent time in his arms, and it hadn't been awful at all. In fact, if she were completely honest with herself—and she always strived to be so—the experience had been wickedly wonderful, and she'd enjoyed it. Enjoyed it far too much. Enjoyed it so much, she wouldn't mind experiencing more of that particular wickedness.

Another wave of self-loathing battered her. How could she even entertain such treacherous thoughts?

6

After a sleepless night of tossing, turning, and the erotic reliving of Gabriella's lush bum pressed to his loins, Max arose with a cockstand to rival Eros's and Pothos's. Deciding an early morning ride before breaking his fast would clear his head and hopefully reduce his state of arousal, he wasted no time in dressing, quite putting Filby out that he'd dared to do so without the valet's assistance.

Thirty minutes later, he slowed Balor, and patting the horse's withers, breathed in the fresh, crisp air. Song birds trilled cheerfully, and a slight breeze rustled the leaves and sent the tall grass to dancing. This was his preferred time of day, when everything was fresh and new, before his responsibilities and duties consumed his hours and thoughts.

As he had last night and continued to do today, he pondered Gabriella's reaction to him. If he didn't know better, he'd suspect she was as attracted to him as he was to her and fought the magnetism just as vehemently. He dared to consider what there could have been between them if the ugly truth of her grandfather's blackmail hadn't caused a permanent wedge.

He turned the stallion toward a favorite copse of oaks growing along the river where he often saw deer early in the morning. There the embankment narrowed to a few feet. As he approached, he canted his head. Someone was singing. More accurately, a female with a lovely alto voice sang *Lavender's Blue*.

He grinned at his good fortune.

Gabriella.

There she sat on the opposite side of the waterway, beyond where the fencing began. Bright as sunshine in a lovely yellow morning gown, her hair tied back with a jonquil ribbon and her straw bonnet beside her. She rested a sketch pad on her knees as she trilled away.

"You must love me diddle diddle,

'Cause I love you..."

She was the most relaxed and unselfconscious he'd ever seen her. And utterly enchanting. With a cluck of his tongue, he urged Balor faster, and the steed soared over the river, landing on the other side.

Unaware of him as yet, with adorable flourish, she swept her pencil across the paper, and neck bent, continued to sing beneath her breath. "*Diddle, diddle*."

He'd like to diddle diddle something. Someone.

"Good morning, Gabriella."

She started, dropped her pencil, and jerked her gaze upward, her mouth forming a delightful little "O" of surprise as she glanced past him. "I didn't hear you approach."

The river and the breeze rustling through the trees could be blamed for that.

He slid to the ground then looped Balor's reins over the pummel. The horse wouldn't wander far. Without waiting for an invitation, Max sank beside her and retrieved her pencil.

"May I see?" He indicated the sketch pad as he handed the pencil to her.

With a little shrug, she passed it over. She'd drawn her grandfather's cattle milling about the meadow, including three newborn calves resting beneath the trees. A robin red breast stood atop a fence post, its head raised in song.

"You have talent," he said returning the pad to her. He wasn't surprised. "You've a lovely singing voice too."

She angled her head at his compliment. "I find drawing relaxes me and is a welcome distraction from things weighing on my mind."

"Like the exchange between your grandfather and me last night?" He gathered her hand in his, fully expecting her to yank it away and renounce him for a bounder and an opportunistic rake.

Instead, she stared at their entwined fingers, hers charcoal-stained. "Yes, that and other things." She slanted her head, contemplatively. "Do you ever wonder what life would have been like if you'd been born a different person?"

Such a serious conversation for so early in the morning. She'd probably fretted all night as well.

"I do on occasion. I'd have much more freedom. There are obligations required of a duke that I don't always relish." Like restoring stolen lands to the duchy and ruining pretty young women's lives in the process. He released her hand before removing his hat and setting it beside his thigh then leaned back on one elbow.

She turned that expressive hazel gaze on him, searching his face. Wistfulness and yearning shone there, and he recognized a kindred spirit. He'd sensed that about her from their initial meeting. Neither would hesitate to do anything for their family. The difference was, his family was dead, whilst her grandparents and her sister lived.

"Honestly, I've never considered there are aspects to being a duke that are difficult or that you disliked." She skewed her mouth in the manner he'd come to recognize meant she was in deep thought. "I've always only thought of the privileges and opportunities your position brings." Gabriella took up her pencil again, but didn't put it to the paper. She seemed lost in ruminations once more.

Today, there was a melancholy air about her, and he yearned to take her in his arms and promise everything would be all right. But he couldn't, because he was going to make her life hell, and part of him wished he'd never found that damned journal.

"I wish that I had been born someone else at times." She pushed a stray tendril of almond-brown hair off her face, leaving a charcoal smudge on her cheek. "Not because I've been unhappy, though I do wish my parents had lived and I'd have known them. But because I'd like to have traveled and seen something of the world. Instead, I expect I'll take care of my grandparents until they pass, and then…?"

"And then?" he probed when she didn't finish.

She hitched a dainty shoulder again, indicating she didn't know what the future would bring.

It was on the tip of his tongue to ask her if she'd never thought of marrying. He checked the question. It wouldn't matter, for he knew her future even if she did not as yet.

"How fares Jackson and your grandmother?" He curled his hand into the grass to keep from grasping her silken locks teasing the mound of her derriere.

"Grandmama is determined to leave her bed today." She frowned at her drawing as she added a bit of shadowing. "And Jackson is resting as well as can be expected. He's in a lot of pain, poor man."

"I arranged to have your grandfather's coach repaired at my expense." Max hadn't intended to mention that. He'd wanted to surprise her. She'd blamed herself for the mishap, though in all honesty, the advanced age of the conveyance was to blame.

One hand half-raised to the wisp of hair flitting about her ear, she glanced at him in open-mouthed astonishment. "Why? He was utterly hateful to you last night. I still burn from mortification at his behavior. I cannot understand it."

"I did it for you, *chérie.*"

Gabriella laid her drawing materials aside then adjusted her position so that she faced him. "Why? You've no reason I can think of to be kind and generous, and to take such actions on my behalf."

So like her. Direct and to the point. Max would seldom have to wonder what went on in her head. She wasn't exactly reticent about telling him, even when it wasn't what he wanted to hear.

I also must ask you, once again, to direct your attentions elsewhere. I am not now, nor will I ever be, receptive to them.

Her words from yesterday hurt, and they ought not to.

He turned her hand over and drew his finger across her palm. "Because I want to be your friend. Possibly, something more."

She stared at him for the longest stretch. It dragged on and on, emotions flitting across her face in rapid succession. At last, she turned her pink mouth down, sighed, and withdrew her hand. "That's not possible, and I think you must know it."

Gabriella averted her gaze, afraid Maxwell would see

the tears pooling in her eyes. She preferred it when he was his usual abominable cocky self, not this tender man. It made her wish for things that could never be.

He rubbed his thumb over her cheek, and she raised her wary gaze to collide with his. "You had a bit of charcoal, just there."

The queerest longing to turn her face into his hand assailed her. Why did he have this power over her? Her head told her he was dangerous. No good. A man not to be trusted. She *knew* that to be true of him as well.

Nevertheless, her fickle heart had taken to him months ago. Gabriella couldn't pinpoint the exact moment she suspected she was more than smitten with his charm and undeniably striking looks. With his smile, his droll wit, and the way his eyes lit up when he was with his friends.

Yes, she did wish she'd been born a different person and that he had been too. Then maybe there would've been a chance for them. As things were now…

"*Chérie*. You're crying."

His awed whisper tumbled her back to the present,

but before she could swipe away the evidence of her upset, he sat up and gathered her into his arms. "What has you distraught?" He murmured into her hair while stroking her back. "Tell me. Mayhap I can help."

No, you cannot.

She should pull away. Slap his face. However, the plain truth was, she didn't want to. Being held in his arms felt the most natural thing in the world, and she'd dreamed of it so often before she'd overheard him that day last December.

He tilted her chin up. "Gabby?" His gaze sank to her mouth, and she was lost.

Leaning in, she grasped his lapel and lifted her mouth in silent invitation. With a strangled groan, he crushed his lips to hers. Lights and flashes exploded behind her eyes, as he nibbled and explored the recesses of her mouth. She looped her arms around his neck, desperate to draw him nearer.

To have this moment, no matter how wrong or how much she'd regret it later.

She breathed Max in, memorizing his scent, the shape of his mouth, the taste of him, the feel of his sculpted form beneath her palms.

He splayed a hand on the small of her back and framed her face with the other. "You are so beautiful." He nuzzled her neck, and she allowed her head to fall back to give him greater access. He skimmed her ribs, his fingers mere inches from her breasts. "Let me call on you, Gabby, and speak to your grandfather about paying my addresses. We could be so good together."

Those words doused her passion as surely as if he'd tossed her into the river sweeping past them a few feet from away. What game did he play?

Jerking away, she pressed her fingers to her throbbing mouth and shook her head so hard her hair ribbon came loose. What was she doing? Had she lost her mind? God, how could she kiss him when she knew what he intended. What kind of a wanton was she? Equally mortified and furious that he'd so easily duped her, she swiftly gathered her drawing materials.

A perplexed frown furrowed his brow. "Gabby…? What's wrong?"

She plopped her bonnet upon her head and scrambled to her feet, standing unsteadily. Shaking, angry at herself for being weak and stupid, and at him for kissing so wonderfully that she'd forgotten who he was, she jutted her chin out.

"I've tried delicacy due to your station being so much more elevated than mine, but at every turn, you continue to press your suit and now have dared to go beyond the mark and kiss me."

"Hold on there." He held up a hand, his tone and expression guarded. "You offered your mouth, and you wanted that kiss as much as I did. Don't you dare deny it."

Scorching heat swept from her breasts to her forehead. "Yes. Yes, I did. My curiosity overcame my common sense, but this was a huge mistake and shan't happen again."

"Are you suggesting you only kissed me out of virginal curiosity?" Curse his noble eyebrow flying high up his forehead in disbelief.

"Of course. What other reason could there be?" *Indeed, Gabriella Fern Miriam Breckensole. What possible reason?*

He rose, all lean, sinewy muscle and animal-like

grace. "You tell me, *chérie.*" His voice as smooth as silk held a dangerous note, and a tremor rattled through her.

"Oh, you are insufferable! Simply impossible. A puffed-up, arrogant toad." She stamped a foot, wishing she had the nerve to kick him in the shin.

He folded his arms and smirked. "Indeed."

"Leave me alone, Your Grace. I mean it."

His smile grew wider and impossibly smugger, and he dared to shake his midnight head.

Itching to lay a palm across his angular face, she presented her back. "I shall give you the Cut Direct. I swear I shall." Though it likely meant goading a bear. Tears made dual tracks down her face as she all but ran from him.

"*Je suis désolé*, *chérie,* but it will make no difference."

7

Four days later, at precisely three of the clock, Gabriella climbed the impressive steps to Ridgewood Court, the Sutcliffes' ducal country house. The afternoon proved one of the lovelier this spring: the temperature pleasant, the sky crystal clear, and the gentlest breeze teasing the new foliage, budding flowers, and the wisps of hair framing her face.

Today, as they did every third Thursday of the month, she and her sister as well as several other of the local gentry not yet in London for the onset of the Season, met for tea and an afternoon of cards. If the weather permitted, guests might take to the lawns for strolls, shuttlecock, or lawn bowling.

Gabriella had deliberately stayed close to home these past days. No trips to Colechester, no evening engagements, and no much-coveted excursions about the countryside either. She'd take no chances of running into the Duke of Pennington. No chances of foolishly indulging in more exquisite kisses that left her senses reeling, and her common sense and indignation fizzled to pathetic embers. She must keep her umbrage fully ablaze to battle her ever-growing attraction to the man.

There was still the musical gathering at the Twisteltons' to sort out. She and Ophelia had already said they were attending, and Nicolette would be disappointed if they cried off now. Gabriella had no idea what excuse she could give Ophelia or their grandparents either. Nevertheless, she had severe second—make that third—thoughts about the wisdom of going since *he* would be there.

Especially given the delivery of two stunning cloaks yesterday: one mazurine blue velvet and labeled "Ophelia" and an emerald green one, with Gabriella's name pinned to the collar. No card accompanied the garments, which caused both grandparents' graying eyebrows to skip about on their wrinkled foreheads.

The conversation replayed in her head, word for word.

"It would seem you girls have an admirer." Grandmama had brushed her fingertips over the fine cloth before slicing them a considering glance. "Do you have any notion who it might be?"

"I haven't a clue, but the cloaks are magnificent. I suppose we must return them," Ophelia had murmured, clearly not liking the idea at all. She brushed her cheek against the fabric, sighing. "Is this similar to the one you ordered for me, Gabby?"

Grandpapa had let that tidbit slip during his rant about the stolen horses, damaged coach, and Pennington's unmitigated gall. Gabriella hadn't intended to mention it and distress her sister.

"Very much so," she had admitted. "But how can we return them, when we don't know who sent them? I suppose we could ask the local seamstresses, but that might prove awkward. Besides, there's no guarantee they were fashioned in Colechester."

Gabriella had a very good idea who was behind the gifts—a very good idea indeed— but she'd bite her tongue in half before voicing her suspicions. She didn't relish another scene with her grandfather and truly feared he'd do something awful, such as torch the gorgeous mantles, if he thought the duke was the benefactor. "I suppose we'll have to donate them."

She hated acknowledging how much that saddened her. Both were utterly exquisite, and she was womanly enough to appreciate the fine workmanship. How the duke had managed to commission them in such a short time bespoke his power and influence. Likely, the seamstress had a much heavier purse for her efforts as well.

Grandpapa poked his head above the week-old newssheet. He'd never pay for a current copy but gladly accepted the papers sent their way from the Sutcliffes and Sheffields. "Could they be a surprise birthday gift from your cousin Everleigh, and the note somehow became lost? It is your first and twentieth birthdays in two days, and certainly the occasion warrants something remarkable."

Ophelia perked up and grabbed Gabriella's hand. "I vow, that must be it! We can ask her at tea tomorrow." At once a frown marred her pretty face. "Though I don't suppose we ought to wear them to tea until we know for certain."

"I must agree, my dear," Grandmama gently said. "I expect your grandfather has the right of it, however."

And so here they were for their monthly tea, Ophelia convinced Everleigh was behind the luxurious gift and Gabriella equally certain the duke was. She'd mentioned the mazurine cloak the day of the coach accident, and she didn't believe in coincidences. If she weren't so blasted annoyed with him, she'd have been touched by the thoughtful gesture. He knew it too, drat the charming rake.

Two reasons had compelled her to accompany Ophelia today. First, the duke had never put in an appearance in all the months Everleigh had hosted the monthly tea, and secondly, the only way to know for certain who sent the mantles was to ask her cousin.

As they reached the top riser, a shiny black coach

bearing a ducal crest rocked to a stop.

Gabriella turned in expectation. Everleigh poked her head out and waved gaily. “Hello, darlings!”

Such a change had come over her since marrying the Duke of Sheffield. She positively radiated happiness these days. Gabriella eyed her cousin’s belly. Was she *enceinte*? Hmm, that might explain the glow.

Everleigh’s step-niece, Rayne Wellbrook followed her descent, and then another young woman Gabriella wasn’t acquainted with stepped onto the courtyard.

Once inside and having been divested of their outerwear, Everleigh smiled and drew the petite, strawberry-blonde forward. “Gabriella and Ophelia, may I introduce Miss Sophronie Slater from the Americas? Her father is one of Sheffield’s business partners. “Ronie, these are my cousins, Ophelia and Gabriella Breckensole.”

Miss Slater offered a shallow curtsy and a bright smile, revealing not quite perfectly straight teeth. Her eyes glinted with excitement. “Everleigh speaks of you often. It’s a pleasure to meet you. My, you are indistinguishable from each other. Did you ever play pranks and switch places?"

Everleigh laughed, whilst shaking a finger at them. "Yes, they did."

Chatting, the five women made their way to the drawing room. At once, Gabriella sensed this was no typical Thursday tea. Far more guests milled about than usually did, and there were several she didn't recognize. She sent Ophelia, a what-is-going-on? look, and her sister lifted her shoulder an inch.

Theadosia spied them and broke into a wide smile. She hurried their way, hands outstretched, the small mound of her belly preceding her.

Gabriella surveyed the room again, and her stomach pitched. *Ballocks and bunions*.

He was here.

There, by the window, too deucedly attractive for her peace of mind. His heated, predatory gaze met hers, and he inclined his sable head. She nearly turned on her heels and headed straight for the carriage. She'd promised to cut him, but Ophelia had already ventured farther into the room with Rayne and Miss Slater.

Gabriella edged near Thea and whispered in her ear. "Why are there so many in attendance today?

Theadosia pressed a hand to her throat and chuckled low. "Well, several of my regulars brought guests. It's a good thing I planned for yard games."

Thirty of the most uncomfortable minutes Gabriella had ever endured passed before she could bear it no longer and begged to be excused to use the necessary. Anything to put distance between herself and Maxwell. Besides, Theadosia and Sutcliffe were about to usher their guests outdoors.

Maxwell hadn't approached her, so perhaps he'd taken her warning to heart. Yet, she knew full well, as did he, she would not cut him here. Not with her sister present. Ophelia would never live down the disgrace. And then she'd have to explain her actions, for neither Theadosia or Everleigh would let such ill-behavior go any more than Nicolette would.

As she made her way to the room set aside for the ladies' personal needs, she frowned. Where was Nicolette?

After splashing a bit of water on her cheeks, then

pinching them to bring a spot of color to her pale face, she stared at her reflection. Though it was two seasons old, her light blue gown complemented her coloring. It did nothing for the haunted look in her eyes, however. She feared the truth of Maxwell's plans must come out sooner than she'd wanted, and then where would she and the rest of her family be?

She closed her eyes and drew in a slow, deliberate breath. *Stop hiding from him. You're made of sterner stuff.* Nonetheless, she chose a meandering route to the lawns where the others had retreated and instead of joining them, took a seat in a sheltered arbor off the terrace.

From there, laughter and calls of encouragement and the occasional muffled curse carried to her on the breeze. What a fine bumblebroth this was. She, the keeper of a dastardly secret and much too interested in the man who could very well ruin her family.

"I wondered where you'd sneaked off to." Without an invitation, Maxwell settled his large frame beside her. What had been a comfortable nook at once became too confined and cramped. His scent filled the small area, and despite her determination not to respond to him, her nostrils quivered and anticipation made her stomach flip-flop.

Gabriella forced herself to inhale and count to ten to compose a civil retort.

"I didn't sneak, and you should not be here." She refused to look at him, for if she did, she would be lost. "And neither should you have sent the cloaks. Grandpapa is convinced Everleigh commissioned them for my sister's and my birthday presents, but I know it was you."

Maxwell neither admitted nor denied the accusation. Leaning back, he stretched his impossibly long, black-clad legs before him. He sighed and eyes closed, rested his head against the back of the arbor. "Thank you for not cutting me."

Sincere or mocking?

Examining him surreptitiously from beneath her half-lowered eyelids, Gabriella tightened her mouth. His thick lashes fanning his chiseled cheekbones couldn't hide the lines of fatigue at the corners of his eyes or the shadows beneath them. She'd like to think the past few days had robbed him of as much sleep as they had her. That he also struggled with his conscience as well as his attraction to her.

"You look tired, Your Grace," she murmured before she could stop herself then silently berated the impulse. He might mistake it for caring or concern.

But she *did* care and that frustrated her to no end. She shouldn't. Not about him.

He cracked his blue eye open, and gave her a long, undiscernible look. Was that regret and tenderness there or was the filtered light playing tricks? *Or…*was she manufacturing what she hoped to see?

"I've had much on my mind," he finally said, opening both eyes.

She made a noncommittal noise then tipped her mouth up at Jessica Brentwood's cry of delight. "I've bested you, Bainbridge," Jessica laughed. "Now you owe me an ice at Gunter's."

"Gabriella?"

The peaceful afternoon had lulled her into a drowsy state. Nights of little sleep might be blamed as well. She hid a yawn behind her hand, knowing she ought to join the others, but unable to muster the energy or the desire to do so. “Hmm?”

“You’ve never explained why you disdain my company.” His usual arrogance was absent. “I can only assume I’ve offended you in some way, and for that I apologize.”

She sighed, wishing she dared tell him all, but afraid to reveal what she knew. Hence, she decided on a different tact. “I see no point in encouraging your interest when we both know nothing can come of it. You’re a duke, and I am a dowerless country miss. There can never be more between us. You are expected to make a brilliant match, and in truth, I am not certain I’ll ever marry.”

“I cannot countenance such a thing,” he said quite forcibly. “You are young and beautiful. Surely you want a home and children.”

The truth of her circumstances couldn’t be denied though her heart ached to think of it. To never know a man’s touch or to carry a child. A flicker of resentment fired in her veins too. She wasn’t nobility, but a gentle-born woman had fewer prospects than the poorest peasant's daughter who might marry for love.

Maxwell covered her folded hands with his, his palm heavy and somehow reassuring. "I don't particularly care about station or dowries." *He is a rarity, then.* "Nor about political connections or expanding my sphere of influence."

Gabriella quirked a skeptical brow and laughed. "I cannot believe that." Not when he was determined to regain Hartfordshire Court at all costs. She twisted to face him. "What do you want from me?" A shocking epiphany danced through her mind, and she narrowed her eyes. "Since a respectable union is beyond our scope, I can only assume you've another, less chivalrous proposition."

It was his turn to look startled, and by Jove, not just a little guilty too. It was in the way he veered his gaze aside for an instant and the distinct rosy hue tinting his sharp cheeks.

By God. She'd made the estimable Duke of Pennington blush.

The air left her lungs in a rush as profound disappointment flooded her. Why she should be surprised he wanted her for his mistress, given what she knew him capable of, she couldn't fathom. But if he'd skewered her with a dagger, her pain would've been less. She tilted her chin up refusing to give her disappointment any power. "I admit, I'd foolishly thought you above such machinations."

She tried to pull her hands away, but he firmed his grip. "You have it wrong." He lifted a hand to his mouth and kissed the back of it, then turned it over to kiss the pulse beating a frantic tattoo at her wrist. "I swear, I would never dishonor you in such a way." Maxwell drew her into his embrace, his gaze locked upon hers. His voice, low and raspy as if intense emotion constricted his throat, he murmured, "You intrigue me as no other ever has."

In less than a blink, his mouth was upon hers, devouring her lips, demanding a response.

Gabriella couldn't deny him, and with a husky moan, twined her arms around his neck and gave in to her hunger.

This was madness. Sweet, wanton, wonderful madness. Her desire for this man would consume her, but in this exquisite sliver of time, she didn't care. Maxwell was here, and she was here, and there was no snuffing the inferno. His kisses went on and on, his tongue dueling with hers, their breath mingling as she lost all sense of anything but him.

A shriek of laughter only a few feet away pierced the heady passion, and this time, Maxwell, drew back, a lopsided smile slashing his mouth. "Forgive me. I lose my self-control the moment I touch you." He traced a finger down her cheek.

She was both delighted and terrified at his admission. Swallowing, her lips throbbing from the sensual onslaught, desire and perhaps something more wrestled with her sense of justice. She couldn't have it both ways. She didn't dare give into whatever this unnamed thing was between them. It would destroy her when—*if*—he claimed Hartfordshire Court.

Male voices echoed on the terrace, and he stood, straightening his waistcoat. "I shouldn't be found here. You would be compromised. But know this, *chérie*, I do not easily give up."

He must be made to do so. But how when every part of her longed to yield to him?

8

The next evening, one shoulder propped against the doorframe to the Twistletons' crowded music room, Max raised his champagne flute to his lips, savoring the quality spirit. From across the span, the Duke and Duchess of Dandridge nodded cheerful greetings as they settled onto the blue-tufted chair cushions. Sutcliffe and Sheffield, along with their magnificent duchesses, had claimed seats for tonight's soiree in the last row of neatly lined chairs.

Swathed in silks and satins, their jewels glittering in the glow of dozens of candles, the ladies resembled brightly-plumaged birds next to the gentlemen's more sedately-hued suits. Only in the human species did the female outshine the male.

Well, most males. The image of a dandified fellow Max had encountered a fortnight ago, attired in pink and canary yellow, intruded upon his musings.

Several other members of *Bon Chance*: The Sinful Lords Secret Society were present as well: Westfall, Bainbridge, and Asherford, dukes one and all, though the organization wasn't limited to dukes, hence the name sinful lords. The group was much more of a brotherhood than a club, a brothel, or gaming hell for debauched aristocrats. It was a place to escape the pressures and responsibilities of having been born a noble. A place where they could just be men. Equals.

A footman placed a violin atop the pianoforte as another arranged a harp just so. Normally, Max eschewed this particular sort of gathering. For a damned good reason too. One never knew what degree of skill those imposed upon to entertain the assembly might claim.

A person with a strong musical inclination himself, he could scarcely sit through the travesties that far too often took to the stage. Usually prompted by a parent oblivious to their progenies' complete and absolute ineptitude.

In London one might fare better, but in the country? No, he'd likely have to sit on his hands to keep from slapping them to his ears. But then how could he cover his mouth to stifle his groans?

Damn him for a fool for accepting tonight.

Forcing an expression other than abject boredom whilst trying to ignore what often amounted to noises similar to mating cats wasn't something he had quite mastered. Nor would he ever. However, he had it on good authority—those very same dukes now murmuring intimately in their wives' ears and from Miss Twistleton herself—that certain twins would indeed be present. He'd had his doubts, and it pleased him no end that after yesterday, Gabriella hadn't forsworn the gathering.

Never had a woman and her mouth held such allure. Or made him incapable of resisting the temptation of being in her presence. Toward that end, he donned his evening finery. Even taking particular care with his appearance and choosing a paisley waistcoat, because the fabric's colors reminded him of her fascinating eyes.

If Max had been prudent, he'd have secured a seat in the back row too. Much easier to make a subtle escape should Gabriella not attend after all. But then, he'd have endured his valet's disapproval over his choice of waistcoat for no good reason.

He finished the superb wine and after combing the room in search of a certain spitfire with dark honey-tinted hair and ever-changing eye color, placed his glass atop the tray carried by a passing hunter green-and-black liveried footman. When offered another flute, he gave a decisive nod. Although truth to tell, it would take three or four *or eight* more to make him less inclined to grimace or yawn during the tedious recitals he anticipated.

A derisive grin quirking his mouth, Ansley, Earl of Scarborough lifted his glass in a silent salute from where he'd positioned himself beside a tall plant. Another member of *Bon Chance*. Unfortunate for Scarborough that he'd chosen this weekend to visit his boyhood home. Since inheriting the earldom from his uncle two years ago, he'd done an admirable job of avoiding social gatherings, and his biting cynicism when forced to appear had earned him the unflattering moniker, the Earl of Sarcasm.

Max returned the gesture, recognizing a kindred soul. Obligation and duty made men do all manner of things they'd prefer not to. Sometimes things which teetered on the precipice of decency and muted their self-respect. Whereas Max more easily controlled his responses to unwanted social interactions, the tic twitching near Scarborough's left eye gave his unease away.

Scarborough's stunning sister, Nicolette Twistleton glided near her brother. She stretched up on her toes, tilted her raven curls toward his dark head, and whispered something in his ear. With a casual shrug, he downed the last of his champagne. Appearing very much like he wished he might indulge in something far stronger, he allowed her to tow him to a front row chair. *Poor, miserable bastard.*

Few people knew Max played the violin, or no doubt, he'd have been imposed upon to entertain this evening as well. He intended to keep that knowledge a secret. He played on a regular basis, but never for others. Not since he'd been fourteen years of age, and he'd eagerly set bow to string for his father whom he hadn't seen in six months. As he was wont to do, the seventh Duke of Pennington had ridiculed rather than praised him before dismissing Max with the aloofness he might've directed toward a tax collector.

Or a clap-ridden whore.

Another casual swallow and with an equally deceptive indifferent scan of the room, Max pulled his mouth taut. A glance to the mantel clock revealed five minutes past eight; the time this grand misadventure was scheduled to have begun. He'd wasted his damned evening, it seemed, for a predictably unpredictable woman. Was there ever a more frustratingly enticing vixen?

Did he dare escape now?

No sense dithering any more of the evening away when his time was better spent perfecting the details of the plan he intended to put into effect soon. Mayhap as shortly as tomorrow, if Gabriella didn't come tonight.

And it certainly seemed she wouldn't.

After Max's encounter with her cantankerous grandfather a week ago, his man of business had paid a call at Chartworth Hall. Struthers brought information quite welcome to Max, but assuredly wouldn't be to that bastard Breckensole. And Gabriella, an unwitting pawn, was paramount to his success.

Actually, she was essential to his preferred plan. The one which showed a degree of mercy and which helped temper his fury with no small amount of sympathy for hers, her twin's, and Mrs. Breckensole's plight. His alternative strategy wasn't as compassionate, and he'd rather not resort to those extremes but would if all else failed.

If *she* failed to cooperate.

He dragged his gaze over the rows of chairs. Thirty in all. It was to be an intimate affair tonight then. At least, according to any society matron worth her salt's standard. He snorted, drawing a curious look from Jessica Brentwood, the Duchess of Sutcliffe's younger sister.

The single woman he'd hope to see, had counted

on seeing, had yet to arrive. Another inspection of the clock revealed nearly half past the hour. Much too late to be considered fashionable. She wasn't coming after all.

Certainly, it wasn't disappointment pinging round and round in his chest much like pebbles shaken in a jar. No, by God. It was annoyance at his own stupidity for having accepted an invitation he oughtn't to have done. And for getting his hopes up after the amazing interlude in the arbor.

And damn his eyes, he couldn't very well leave before the first person performed and still remain in his influential hostess's good graces. Invitations must keep coming, and he must know which functions Gabriella would also attend.

When another discreet inspection of the assembled guests failed to locate the attractive female he sought, he brushed his fingers along his jaw. Sutcliffe's gaze met his, and Max raised a questioning eyebrow. *Where is she?*

Sutcliffe hitched a shoulder before bending his ear to his wife once more. He was of no help whatsoever, besotted fool.

Had Mrs. Breckensole's health taken a turn for the worse again, keeping her granddaughters at home? Max had spoken with Dr. Spratt two days ago, and the capable physician had assured him that Mrs. Breckensole recovered nicely.

Why he should be so anxious for Gabriella's presence, he refused to examine. He would have Hartfordshire Court, one way or another. Her cooperation simply lessened the hardship for her sister and grandmother. He didn't give a tinker's damn about *lessening* Breckensole's shock.

It hadn't escaped Max that Gabriella had avoided answering his question the other night. It also hadn't escaped him that she'd been appalled at her grandfather's frothing antagonism. Her reaction only confirmed what he'd suspected all along. None of the Breckensole women had any notion what Harold Breckensole had done. What the scapegrace continued to do.

An unfamiliar sensation constricted Max's chest and burned the back of his throat. If he were a better man, a kinder more forgiving man, he'd let the issue of Hartfordshire Court's ownership go. After all, the Breckensoles had resided there for decades. Surely the comfortable house was the only home Gabriella and her sister could remember.

Didn't she—they—deserve clemency? Their grandfather's sins weren't theirs. They shouldn't have to suffer because of his reprehensible decisions.

Max's eyes drifted shut for a blink, and the gaunt, haunted features of his opium-addicted grandfather burst into his mind. An image straight from the bowels of hell. No, dammit. Breckensole had done that to Grandfather. He may not have tipped the laudanum-laced whisky into a glass every day, but he'd stolen the one thing that meant the most to the old man.

Grandmother.

And the repercussions had been far reaching. Grandfather had become a man incapable of loving, or perhaps afraid to show affection to his only child. It had also made him powerless to resist the alcohol and opium that numbed his senses and blotted unbearable memories from his mind. As a result of his lack of love and approval by his sire, Max's father's soul had warped and twisted as well, and Max had been the recipient of *his* cruelty.

But what of Mrs. Breckensole? What of the twins? That common sense voice prodded his conscience for at least the hundredth time. Until he wanted to shout every foul oath he knew, and the incessant nagging still didn't stop. *They are innocent in this. Must they suffer in order for me to dole out vengeance? Especially as the offense wasn't against me?*

He quaffed back the rest of his champagne and soundly quashed his ruminations. Sometimes, when righting wrongs, other blameless parties had to suffer. That was just the way of it. Lest he forget, he reminded himself severely, Grandmother and the babe she'd carried had been innocents too.

"What has you looking so Friday-faced, Pennington? Downright glum, I might add."

Max slid Crispin, Duke of Bainbridge a quizzical glance then looked pointedly at the punch cup he held—no doubt liberally dosed with brandy or whisky from the flask always in Bainbridge's pocket.

"I never look Friday-faced, Bainbridge. I'm simply hoping tonight's entertainment proves more enjoyable than the last musical I attended." That had proved so dreadful, he'd abstained for five years. When he closed his eyes, he could still hear Amelia Johnson's off-key—*very, very off-key*—trilling and see her bursting into tears and fleeing the room when an insensitive, foxed-to-his-fleshy-gills clod pate tottered inside, snickered loudly, and asked where he might view the atrociously singing parrots.

"Of course you don't," Bainbridge put forth drolly. "So that downturned mouth and your gaze straying to the entrance every few seconds, not to mention the two glasses of champagne you've consumed already, means you're a cheerful chap?" he quipped as he slapped Max's shoulder.

"Stubble it, Bainbridge. You are no keener on these sorts of husband-hunting assemblies than I am. In fact, I'm surprised to see so many of our set here. I'd have thought they'd all be in London by now preparing for the Season." However, since Max had determined who his duchess would be, albeit for all of the wrong reasons, he needn't concern himself with the marriage-minded mamas here or in Town.

Bainbridge drew his sober attention from his study of the lovely Jessica Brentwood and offered another wry smile. "No small amount of truth there. But one has to have something to do on these tediously endless days until Parliament is in session and the Season officially begins. I'm not given to stalking and fishing, and even I grow a trifle bored with my horse breeding venture. I dare say, once the mare is impregnated, it's just a matter of waiting, is it not?"

"You're babbling, Bainbridge."

"Not a bit of it. If you're looking for the Breckensoles, I have it on good authority that they'll be arriving with Rayne Wellbrook and Justina Farthington. Miss Farthington's dragon of an aunt, Emily Grenville will likely play chaperone to the foursome for the evening." Bainbridge cocked his head, running a long finger the length of his champagne glass. "You do know Breckensole's coach was wrecked and villains stole his team. And Gabriella was only spared because she most prudently hid in the woods?"

Max closed his eyes until they were mere slits. Since when did Bainbridge address Gabriella by her first name? Christ on the Sabbath. Did *he* have a *tendre* for her?

What a distasteful notion. That one of the gentlemen he called friends might have a romantic interest in her galled. Except the way Bainbridge's regard kept straying to the fair Jessica Brentwood suggested his interest lay in another direction.

Good.

Max couldn't very well play his hand just yet and announce he intended to leg shackle himself to Gabriella. Thank God he found her attractive—*too deucedly luscious*—and keen of intellect. But even if she'd resembled a goose's hind end, had the protruding teeth of a buck-toothed hare, and possessed the acumen of a turnip, it would've changed nothing.

Well, the begetting an heir might have proven more of challenge had that been the case. Even dosed with spirits and in a pitch-black bedchamber, one needed a strong constitution to even consider that tedious task if the female weren't desirable. He needn't worry on that account, by God.

No, bedding Gabriella Breckensole wouldn't be a chore he forced himself to perform for the duchy's sake. He'd enjoy it as a man very much drawn to her softly rounded curves would. As a man who'd wanted her almost from the first minute he'd met her. Contemplating her warming his bed, desire tingled through his veins, a mellow, burgeoning warmth.

His body responded predictably, most inconveniently—damned his erotic musings. With deliberate intent, he turned his thoughts to her despicable grandsire and succeeded in curbing his arousal quite handily.

Gabriella wouldn't like what Max was about. In fact, he could all but guarantee her outrage, but wed him she would. And be glad for the opportunity when he explained the alternative.

"Pennington? Did you hear me? Wreck? Villains? Woods?" From the sardonic smirk twisting Bainbridge's mouth, he well knew Max had.

"Yes, I'm aware," Max admitted, giving him a

moody smile. "I'm the one who saw her home. Rescued her driver too."

Except for the slightest lifting of one eyebrow, Bainbridge did a remarkable job of keeping his surprise contained.

A commotion at the door announced the onset of more guests.

"The Breckensole twins have arrived at last," Bainbridge offered needlessly.

The five late-comers burst in amid apologies, laughs, and heartfelt greetings.

At once, Gabriella's inquisitive gaze met Max's, almost as if she'd searched for him upon entering as he had for her this half hour past. He lifted his glass and brows simultaneously in a silent salute.

Resplendent in a chaste white gown adorned with cherry-colored ribbons and an embroidered overskirt, she outshone every other woman present. The candlelight caught the whispers of golden-bronze threading her hair and made her skin gleam with a pearly effervescence. Her berry red lips parted slightly in the tiniest of hesitant smiles, tipping those rosebud lips upward, before she drew her regard away. Nevertheless, wariness and distrust yet tinged her thick-lashed eyes when she regarded him.

Disappointment stabbed, chinking at his pride. For God's sake. What had he expected? That she'd suddenly welcome his company after months of avoiding him?

Yes, dammit. That's precisely what he'd expected.

At the very least a slight warming after he'd rescued her and helped her injured coachman. Most assuredly after he'd inconvenienced himself and ridden to Colechester to fetch the doctor. He'd gone so far as to make sure Mrs. Breckensole's every medical need was met at his expense.

Not that the Breckensoles were aware of that last bit. He wouldn't put it past Breckensole to refuse out of pride and spite. Max felt obligated to pay the fees after a lengthy, enlightening chat with Mr. Armstrong Edgeman, the brother of this evening's hostess, had revealed Breckensole's finances were in dun territory.

But mainly, he'd anticipated a favorable response because of the stirring kisses he'd shared with

Gabriella.

Oh, she'd done the pretty in her feminine and flowing handwriting. She'd sent 'round a politely worded note thanking him for his assistance. It hadn't escaped him that she made the gesture and not her grandfather. Her perfectly worded missive held no hint of the sensual vixen he'd kissed more than once.

Her twin, also wearing a frothy white gown, only Miss Ophelia's bore lavender-toned accents, immediately swept to Miss Twistleton's side.

"May I have your attention, please?" Beaming, Mary Twistleton stood at the front of the room and clapped her hands twice drawing everyone's attention. "Please do have a seat. Now that everyone is here, we may begin the evening's entertainment. I'm sure you will be well-pleased." She swept a gloved hand toward the Breckensoles. "Ophelia and Gabriella have kindly agreed to lead off with a rendition of *Sonata for Violin and Piano in B Minor* by Johann Sebastian Bach."

Ah, they were part of the evening's entertainment. No wonder the party hadn't begun on time. Heaven forbid the order of performances be changed to accommodate late arrivals. Max took in Scarborough's stiff mien and realization struck. For his sake, his mother couldn't adjust the agenda. To do so would completely disconcert the earl, a man who held to rigid routines and schedules. Sympathy again washed him for the other man's plight.

"My son, the Earl of Scarborough and my daughter Nicolette will follow with Mozart's *Sonata in C*." Her proud, but fond gaze rested on her children for an instant before she flicked her elderly father a rather strict warning glance and then motioned expectantly to the guests still standing. Her brother, the banker, was noticeably absent. "Plenty of seats remain. Please find one."

Not exactly plenty.

Max waited as the others obediently filed to their places. All except the Breckensole twins. After bussing their hostess's cheek and exchanging swift hugs with her, they made their way to the pianoforte.

Other than their attire, the women appeared identical, and it never ceased to flummox him that while he appreciated Ophelia's loveliness, he'd never felt the slightest jot of attraction to her. Her sister on the other hand, had him in a constant state of arousal. That truth irritated as much as confounded.

He didn't hail from a family given to emotion or impulse, although he'd always had a devil of a time reining in his sense of humor. Nonetheless, he didn't like or appreciate his unfettered responses to Gabriella. They fogged his mind, muddled his intentions, and that he could not permit.

Ophelia settled gracefully onto the bench before the grand instrument, and his jaw loosened the slightest in astonishment when Gabriella collected the violin from atop the polished mahogany.

She played the violin? A pleased smile ticked his mouth upward. By Jove. They had something in common after all. Ridiculous that he should be so delighted at something so inconsequential. At once he desired to play Bach's *Concerto for Two Violins* with her. Perchance after they were wed…

Eyes narrowed slightly, he took note of the remaining seats. Another small, satisfied grin curving his mouth at his good fortune, he made his way to three unoccupied chairs in the front row. One was undoubtedly intended for their bubbly hostess. The others…

Without a pang of compunction, he claimed the pair for himself and Gabriella.

Her eyes rounded the merest bit as she shifted her gaze between him, the empty seat to his right, and the only two other unoccupied chairs in the room. Her mouth, a sweet, prim line of reproach, she looked pointedly to *those* vacant chairs.

Her expressive gaze fairly screamed, "*Move*!"

Not on his life. He gave a slight shake of his head.

Her eyelids lowered the merest bit, and her acute gaze promised vengeance and a proper dressing down. A perverse thrill scuttled up his spine. Oh, Miss Gabriella Breckensole was a worthy opponent, to be sure.

He cocked an eyebrow, crossed one leg over the other, and tipped his mouth upward in a silent challenge. *Do your worst, love.*

Fairly bristling with indignation, her eyes grew dark and smoky. Just as swiftly, her features softened into a benign mien, but she couldn't quite subdue the sparks spewing from her gaze. She'd happily plant him a facer, he hadn't a doubt.

Something—surely not guilt or remorse or a misplaced sense of integrity—scuffed hard and abrasive against his need for revenge. A lesser man might've quelled under her blistering stare. Beneath the knowledge that he was a manipulative blackguard. Yet he didn't move.

It wouldn't do to switch places now, in any event. After all, the presentation was about to begin, and indisposing the other guests and further delaying the performances would be most inconsiderate of him. Or so he assured himself.

Bastard, his conscience railed. *Knave. Cretin.* Jaw taut, he stifled his recriminations then dispassionately lifted a shoulder as if to say, "*It's too late now, chérie.*"

Up went Gabriella's chin; a sure sign he'd further aroused her ire. But unless she wanted to crawl across the laps of the other guests and claim the lone chair in the middle of the third row, she'd have to join him in the front. Well, she might take the chair beside Jessica Brentwood, but he'd vow Miss Brentwood had saved it particularly for Ophelia. Everyone knew they shared a special friendship.

Ophelia played a few opening chords, hauling his wayward musings back to the present, and the audience settled into a polite—perhaps the tiniest bit strained—silence.

Slightly angling away from the rows of guests, Gabriella lifted the violin to her chin. For several unexpectedly pleasant minutes, only the sound of the sisters' expert playing filled the room, and he found himself lost in Bach's hauntingly beautiful tune.

Gabriella played with grace and passion. Eyes closed, her lashes trembling every now and again as she swayed in time, emotions flitted across the smooth planes of her alabaster face.

That the twins practiced together often was apparent and that they'd had superb instructors, equally so. Their grandfather permitting the sisters this luxury astonished him. More than a little, truth be told. It seemed when it came to his granddaughters,

Breckensole wasn't a complete and utter arse. The old sod reserved that characteristic for nearly everyone else.

Max found himself humming along, his fingers itching to play his violin. He didn't close his eyes, for he couldn't bear to tear his gaze from Gabriella.

The last note faded away, and after a brief, rather stunned silence, the audience interrupted into enthusiastic applause and calls of approval. Pink tinging their cheeks, the sisters dipped curtsies and after Gabriella set aside her violin, they made their way to the seats.

"Ophelia." Miss Brentwood patted the chair beside her. "Sit here. I saved it especially for you."

Just as Max had suspected.

With a questioning glance to her twin, Ophelia paused, obviously worried about deserting her sister. She had no choice. No other two seats were available together. He'd seen to that; God rot his black soul.

An affectionate smile bending her mouth, Gabriella nodded whilst giving her twin a little shove in the back. "Go along."

Fingering her fan, she faced him. She could either sit beside him or disrupt the third row. With a resigned sigh, only decipherable if one studied her closely, she claimed the chair to his right and promptly flicked her painted, lace-edge fan open. And snapped it shut. Open. Shut. Open. Shut. *You are cruel.*

He almost laughed aloud at her silent, terse message. Instead, tenser than he ought to be, he watched to see if she'd draw the frilly accessory through her hands. That meant *I hate you.*

Staring straight ahead, she didn't move except for the rhythmic rising and falling of her chest, the slow blinking of her expressive eyes, and the *tap-tap, tap-tap of* her slippered toes. Nonetheless, he felt the vexation radiating from her. A doubt didn't exist she'd love to have snubbed him once more. Instead, she'd sunk onto the blue-cushioned seat with the aplomb of a queen and disregarded him as if he were a lowly boot-shine boy.

Her decision revealed an aspect of her character he'd already suspected she possessed and which played perfectly into what he intended to do to regain

Hartfordshire Court. Miss Gabriella Breckensole would suffer rather than cause others discomfort or inconvenience. That he would exploit the goodness in her for his own mean ends said much about him for all of his professions that he was a gentleman.

"Well done, Miss Breckensole," Charles Edgeman, Mrs. Twistleton's aged father, a retired banker, whispered loudly on her other side. More than a little deaf, Edgeman was wont to bellow when he believed himself inconspicuous. "I quite enjoyed your performance. One of the best I've heard, I do believe."

Once more, color climbed the slopes of her ivory cheeks, but Gabriella demurred with a kind smile and bowed head. "You are most kind, Mr. Edgeman."

"I quite agree," Max murmured. "Is there anything you don't do well?"

"Hold my tongue when you are about," she snapped, a false smile painted upon her lips.

Which only made him want to kiss the soft pillows until a seductress's smile bent her mouth. Her fresh fragrance tickled his nose, and he inhaled deeply. Yes, definitely a hint of lemon, lavender, and jasmine. An interesting, heady, and unexpected *mélange*. Much like her.

Scarborough, looking crosser than a scorpion caught by the tail, and his vivacious sister perched side-by-side on the bench. Miss Twistleton whispered something to her brother, and his features softened a trifle. He even deemed to twist his mouth into a half-smile.

Max hadn't any sisters. Not a brother either. He'd often wondered what it would've been like to have another child to keep him company. Maybe he wouldn't be turning into a cold, unfeeling bastard, not so different from his father, after all.

"Happy birthday, Miss Breckensole," he murmured softly. "Did you and your sister get your gifts?"

She gave him a reproachful glance, marked uncertainty shadowing her expression. "Fishing for praise? I already told you that we did, and I thank you. But surely you know full well it's improper, and we cannot keep them.

"Ah, yes, in the arbor. I forgot." He hitched a

shoulder. "No one but you and I know where they came from."

"The seamstress knows," she all but hissed beneath her breath.

"Ah, but she's in London, and doesn't know who they were for."

"You are impossible," she muttered with a little shake of her head, causing her earrings to bob.

"So you've remarked before." From the side of his mouth he whispered, "I didn't know you played the violin."

"I should think there are a great many things you do not know about me, Your Grace," came her equally hushed but acerbic retort. She tilted nearer a fraction. "Cats make me sneeze. I abhor fish of any sort, most especially shellfish, and I don't take milk with my tea. I cannot resist maid of honor tarts, I enjoy long walks and sketching, and I have a distinct dislike for bullies and liars."

Touché, chérie.

"Now do be quiet, Duke. We're being most rude." A censuring sideways glance accompanied that pert comment.

He hid a grin. If any woman could bring him up to mark, if he cared to be brought up to mark that was, it would've been Gabriella Breckensole. Appearances mattered to her. He'd already garnered that truth. Another factor in his favor.

Scarborough's and his sister's fingers whisked back and forth upon the keys, and under cover of the music Max murmured in Gabriella's shell-like ear, "I should like to call upon you tomorrow. To take you for a carriage outing."

So swiftly did she whip her neck to gawk at him, she nearly smacked his head.

Another delighted chuckle threatened to escape. Her strong reaction was sure to have drawn attention, and only sheer will prevented him from turning to see who'd noticed her shock. He didn't want the gossip starting just yet.

Her pretty, pink mouth parted in astonishment, she stared as if he'd sprouted several more noses or eyes or a pecan-sized boil on his chin. The colliding of their gazes proved astonishingly intense, and lingering far too long for propriety, had a surge of sensual awareness slamming into him.

Merde, but if she didn't put him off his stride like no other.

He did venture a swift, casual glance around. As he suspected, a few guests peered at them curiously. With an insouciance he was far from feeling, he affected a mien of ennui, and ever so slowly, focused his attention on the infuriated woman beside him.

The music grew to a frenzy, and she snapped her mouth shut even as green flecks sparked in her eyes once more. She faced forward.

"No."

That was it. No niceties to temper the rejection. No explanation. Just *no*, which revealed she'd erected her battalions once more.

He leaned nearer, staggered at the self-loathing spearing his gut at the moment. He really was a ruthless, bloody cad. "Yes. You will, my dear. Because I have the means to ruin your grandfather, and only you can decide which course I'll take. Utter annihilation or a mite more benevolent bend."

9

Pacing the length of the bridge for at least the seventh time, Gabriella checked her watch. She'd deliberately arrived fifteen minutes early in order to make sure the Duke of Pennington didn't do as he'd vowed last night and call upon her at Hartfordshire Court.

His arrival was sure to send Grandpapa into an apoplexy and Grandmama back to her sick bed. Ophelia, on the other hand, would be agog with curiosity and sure to ask a myriad of questions Gabriella either had no answers for or was unwilling to reveal.

How she despised lying to her grandparents and

sister, but this was better. She could discover exactly what the duke schemed and determine what troubles he plotted, and how to best foil his ominous plans.

She swung around and marched back over the cobblestones, the clacking of her sensible half-boots a welcome distraction to the tumultuous thoughts roiling about in her head. Clutching her sketch-pad and pencil case she glowered at the undeserving ground.

Oh, how tempted she'd been to give him a proper set down and cut him as she'd threatened to do, but then thought better of it. It behooved her to stay in his good graces, even if his opinion meant less to her than the terrified mouse that had scrambled across the road a bit ago as she tramped down the drive

Just when she had thought—*hoped*—that perhaps there was a streak of decency in the Duke of Pennington, that she might be able to approach him, and perchance strike a bargain, he'd resorted to heavy-handed tactics once more. Weighty and bitter disappointment fueled her anger. He'd left her with no choice but to agree to see him today. She'd much rather have told him to go bugger the devil.

Stupid. Stupid. Stupid.

The very first thing she'd done upon entering the Twistletons' was to search him out. As if seeing him in person would erase the hours he'd consumed her thoughts. And not just because of his vile intentions.

No, other things kept sifting into her mind: their meeting in the arbor. His strong hands encircling her waist. The almost sensual brush of his thighs cradling her bum as she rode before him. His warm breath caressing her ear as he whispered to her. And his crisp, alluring manly scent which she could still smell if she closed her eyes. And hardest to erase from her memory, his wonderfully, delicious mouth upon hers.

Her lids drifted downward, and with a little start, she popped them wide open again.

She most certainly wasn't indulging in daydreams about the insufferable man or how magnificent he smelled. Or the queer way her body responded to him. Indeed, she was not. She forbade it. The foolish optimism she'd allowed after their meeting in the arbor had evaporated, leaving her disillusioned and all the more distrustful.

Face lifted to the sun's soothing rays, she wrestled her ire and attraction under control. At least the weather had cooperated, and for that small reprieve she was grateful. When she'd declared she was off for a lengthy stroll on this fine spring morning, her sketchpad in hand, no one had quirked so much as an eyebrow. She took frequent walks, often drawing birds and other wildlife she happened upon.

Today, she daren't ask Ophelia to come along as a chaperone, else her sister be pulled into the dishonest charade as well. Besides, her twin had a headache and wanted to recover before having tea with Jessica Brentwood this afternoon. Gabriella had cried off joining them.

Head lowered she gave an unfortunate stone a vicious kick.

One hour.

That was precisely how long she would allow Pennington to explain himself before she demanded that he return her here. It had taken all of her self-restraint not to bolt from the Twistletons' last night. But that would've given rise to gossip, and intuition told her there was already going to be enough tongue wagging. Nearly everyone had seen her reaction, and several of her friends and her sister had questioned her about it when the performances ended and the guests were enjoying the tasty refreshments.

Gabriella had laughed off her response, claiming she'd been startled when the duke revealed he, too, played the violin. It pleased and annoyed her that they had that in common. A smug smile arced her mouth. She'd made sure that tidbit made the rounds. He'd not get off lounging like a great, spoiled cat in the audience next time.

Still, she'd been obligated to sit beside him for the next interminable hour, her mind a cacophony of raucous thoughts and worry and what very well might've been despair. If anyone had asked her impression of a single performance, she couldn't have answered truthfully. Thank God, no one had. Only, she'd bet her best gown, because her startling reactions to Pennington had piqued far more interest than anything she might have had to say about the recital.

Ophelia, on the other hand, had noticed. From the

tiny vee pulling her fine eyebrows together, she didn't believe Gabriella's tarradiddle. She'd never been particularly astute at fibbing. Her eyes usually gave her away, as she hadn't mastered the ability to look directly into someone's face and lie through her teeth. Pennington suffered no such qualm, she'd be bound.

But was she so very different? After all, she'd been lying to him for months now, and yet she didn't believe the flaw was a permanent black spot upon her character.

Closing her eyes, she drew in a long, slow breath, counting to ten then reversed the procedure and breathed out slowly, counting to ten again. She repeated this process three times, and on each inhalation and exhalation firmly instructed herself to remain calm and in control. To employ wisdom. To use her wit and intellect. She would—*oh, God, I must*—find a way out of this conundrum.

How, she couldn't conceive.

A trio of ducks emerged from under the bridge, joining another half dozen or so farther along the embankment. Any other day, she would've been eager to sketch them. The crunching of wheels upon gravel alerted her to a vehicle. A smart gig approached from the direction of Chartworth Hall, and even with the sun reflecting off the shiny ebony lacquer, her heart sank impossibly further. The Duke of Pennington tooled the vehicle himself.

Of course he did

Hmm. Eyes narrowed, she tapped her toe. Had the duke anticipated she'd come by herself? He must have, because the gig only accommodated two occupants. She nearly swore aloud, realizing he'd outfoxed her. *Confound it.* She thought *she'd* outwitted him by meeting him on the bridge. She had the most childish urge to stick her tongue out and stomp her foot.

She'd anticipated a coachman or an outrider to observe at least a degree of propriety.

There was nothing for it, however. Pennington would have his say. She'd have hers. And perhaps, just perhaps, an amiable solution might be reached. Truth to tell, she hadn't much hope of that. But it was worth a try, at least. She *must* try. If she didn't punch him in his noble, perfectly straight aristocratic nose first.

Wise to control her fuming temper then, but how he infuriated her. He maneuvered to force her to sit beside him last night and then oh, so smoothly announced that if she refused to accompany him today, he'd proceed with ruining Grandpapa.

That he could turn so cold and mercenary after the kisses they shared, bewildered and wounded her. As he drew the magnificent cream-colored, black-maned mare to a stop, Gabriella didn't even try to conceal her scowl. If she weren't so irritated with the duke, she would've taken a moment to pet the gorgeous creature.

"Good morning, Gabriella." His simple greeting contained warmth, a hint of wariness, and perchance even a tinge of regret.

Giving her his tummy-fluttering smile that no doubt worked to woo other ladies of his acquaintance, he doffed his top hat. After he placed it back upon his midnight hair, he jumped to the ground with agile ease. Adorned in dove gray trousers, his muscular thighs flexed with the motion. His navy coat strained tight across ridiculously wide shoulders, and she cursed herself for noticing.

Under the brim of his hat, his eyes almost looked the same color. Did their different shades ever bother him? Why did she care? She didn't, of course.

"I must return home within the hour, Your Grace, else my grandparents will become suspicious or worried. I told them I was going for a walk and to sketch." For emphasis, she wobbled her pad and pencils as she eyed the gig knowing full well she wouldn't be able to climb aboard without his assistance.

Gabriella didn't want him to touch her again. Her mind and body reacted in all kinds of silly girlish, foolish ways when he did. She must keep her faculties about her today, for she had but one chance to deter him from whatever he planned to do.

He swept a gloved hand toward the conveyance. "Shall we, then?"

No, we should not.

With a nod, just this side of petulant, she approached the vehicle. He took her pad and pencils and placed them on the seat. With the effortlessness of a man accustomed to physical exertion, he grasped her waist and easily lifted her into the gig.

Determinedly ignoring her frolicking stomach, she gathered her drawing supplies and claimed a spot. She scooted as far away from him as the bench allowed—a whole three inches. Knowing him, he'd probably chosen this conveyance precisely because the seat was so narrow.

The vehicle tipped as he sprang aboard, and after he collected the reins, he gave them a gentle shake and clucked his tongue. "Walk on, Aphrodite."

With a swish of her majestic ebony tail, the mare ambled forward.

He *would* have a mare named after the goddess of fertility. And love. And passion.

Do shut up!

Rather than proceeding toward Colechester, the duke steered the horse into a semi-circle, and headed back toward Chartworth Hall.

Gabriella glanced behind them before facing forward and knitting her brow. She fiddled with the edge of her sketch pad. "Why are we traveling this way? There's more to see in the other direction."

Pennington slid her a sideways look, an undefined smile kicking his mouth up on one side. "Because there's a secluded grove on my estate away from the main house where I am assured we'll have privacy, and no one will overhear us. You know the one. It's across from where I met you the other day."

She wasn't sure whether to be more shocked at his suggestion, infuriated by his brazenness, or worried for her virtue. She chose the latter. Giving a sharp shake of her head, her bonnet's pink ribbons flying around her chin, she drew herself up. "I've already risked my reputation by being alone with you. I shan't accompany you to some clandestine location where any number of things might happen."

The thick arcs of his lashes masking his half-closed eyes, he remained silent for a long, uncomfortable slice of a moment before nodding. "I take your point, Gabriella, but we can hardly have this conversation in the middle of the lane. And I *am* considering your reputation." He had the nerve to flash that cocky smile and wink.

She almost growled in annoyance.

"Besides, lest you forget, we've been alone several times, including the other night. I do believe your sitting before me on the saddle was much more scandalous than this sedate ride or our interlude in the arbor."

Tapping her toes in irritation, a frustrated growl did throttle up her throat, but she firmly squelched it. *Stay calm. Do not let him upset you. This isn't just about you. Think of your family.* Nevertheless, Gabriella struggled for cool composure, only achieving a semblance of poise after inhaling and exhaling to a count of ten.

"Your Grace, I remind you once more." *Gads, but the man could be obtuse.* "I haven't given you leave to use my Christian name. And as for this conversation, does it matter where we have it?" She flung a hand in the air. "You know as well as I that few people travel this track. Furthermore, if you were indeed concerned about my repute, why ever did you kiss me before or arrive in this?" She spread both hands to indicate the conveyance they sat in. On the other hand, a coach might've had a driver, but they'd have been enclosed inside, out of everyone's sight.

Perhaps… Perhaps this was the wiser choice, after all. How that truth vexed her that he'd likely considered that aspect when she had not.

Rather than answer, Pennington continued along the road, little puffs of dust rising with each step the mare took. *By Jupiter.* Did he intend to ignore her?

Anxiety knotted her shoulders and stomach, and she pressed a hand to her middle. Mayhap she should have broken her fast with something more substantial than tea. She wasn't afraid exactly. Not of him, or what he might do to her. He'd had the chance to ravish her on more than one occasion, and except for his scalding kisses and that ear nuzzling business, he hadn't pressed unwanted attentions upon her. Even those didn't count, since she'd enjoyed them.

No, what assailed her now was fear of the unknown. She *knew* he wanted Hartfordshire Court. She also appreciated he wasn't above using any means to obtain the estate. What she didn't know, was what role did she play in his plans? Why did he continue to woo her?

She alternated tapping her feet as the wheels' crunching and soft *clop-clop* of Aphrodite's hooves accented the strained silence between them. A goshawk cried overhead, and a grayish-brown hare, one ear raised in caution, paused in its watchful journey across the grassy meadow. The hawk screamed again, and the hare darted beneath a nearby bush.

Gabriella well knew how the poor creature felt. This weighty silence and anticipating whatever Pennington wanted to say plucked at her tattered nerves like an out of tune violin.

An unladylike snort nearly escaped her at the bad comparison.

"There's a place just a little bit further along where we can stop near the river," Pennington finally said. "It's visible from the road but will allow us a degree of privacy."

Twisting on the seat, she faced him. "I don't understand why you don't just tell me what is on your mind. Last night, you threatened to ruin my grandfather, and I know you're plotting to take

Hartfordshire Court from him. I overheard you at the Sutcliffes' house party."

There. Let him make of that what he would. She'd been burning to confront him with the truth for days now. He'd find she was no reticent miss, willing to sit by and watch him destroy her family. She'd not make this easy on him.

A vaguely nonplused look skittered across his face, and she swore red tinged his angular cheeks. "*That's* why your behavior toward me changed," he murmured. Something akin to pain or regret seeped into his tone and glinted in his eyes.

How dare *he* seem hurt? *He* was the one scheming to destroy her family. To take their home. So firmly did she grip her pencil case, her knuckles turned white. Only counting to ten kept her from releasing the full fury of her tongue upon him.

His chest expanded with a deeply drawn breath as he steered the mare off the road and down the mildly sloping meadow to the river. He better not suggest this was difficult for him too. By Jove, she *would* plant him a facer if he even hinted at such a preposterous thing.

Gabriella remained obstinately silent. She'd not absolve him nor would she continue to entreat him to explain himself. A harpy, she was not.

Once the duke had brought the gig to a stop, he cleared his throat, and after removing his hat and gloves and propping them atop one thigh, scraped his long fingers through those dark sable strands. They glinted the merest bit coppery in the sunlight. "I truly regret you overheard that exchange, Gabriella. And even more so, I apologize for the angst you must've endured these past months." Genuine contrition deepened his voice to a mellow purr, and instead of going all prickly as she ought to, Gabriella cursed herself for softening toward him.

Dangerous. Very, very dangerous.

And yet, she had no idea how to respond. She'd expected vehement denials or excuses, not what seemed very much a heartfelt apology. Certainly not that he cared about her feelings or that he felt remorse she'd been worried frantic.

So, she chose boldness and to go on the offensive as the wisest tactic. "Why are you determined to wrest our home from us? What does my accompanying you today have to do with your ruining my grandfather? And pray tell, how could you possibly conceive that I would aid you in any way, knowing what I do?"

He relaxed against the seat and holding his hat and gloves in place, propped one booted foot on the edge of the gig then braced a forearm across his bent knee.

She scowled, steering her avid attention from the interesting bulge at his loins, made prominent by his casual repose. He certainly appeared well-endowed. Mortification consumed her at her wanton thoughts. Why must he appear so dratted manly, so deuced attractive even in this situation?

Maxwell's signet ring glinted in the sunlight as he rubbed his fingertips together. Surely he wasn't anxious as well? He was a duke. *A duke!* A man accustomed to power and privilege. All he had to do was snap his manicured fingers and just about anything he desired was his. The ludicrous concept that *he* was uncertain, bewildered her. She knew him capable of tenderness and kindness. She'd witnessed it and had personally experienced his gentleness.

He stopped fidgeting and laid his hand flat on that absurdly well-formed knee. "I have evidence—indisputable evidence, mind you—that your grandfather cheated my grandfather. Then he blackmailed my grandfather into selling him Hartfordshire Court, which had been my grandmother's familial home for generations."

She choked on a gasp, her gaze flying to his face. "No. That's utterly absurd. Simply not possible." Her sketchpad and pencils slid to the floor as she clasped a hand to her throat. "I don't believe you." Gabriella slowly shook her head.

Don't or cannot? Or…shan't?

An excruciatingly minute inched by before he hitched a shoulder, his gaze trained somewhere beyond the frothing river. "Whether you believe me or not, it is the truth. I have irrefutable proof. As a result of your grandfather's shady dealings, my heartbroken and pregnant grandmother died."

No. No. He fabricated that codswallop. Grandpapa wouldn't. But—

She shook her head again, as much in denial of his

words as her unbidden, perfidious thoughts.

"A shattered man, incapable of loving anyone afterward—including my father—my grandfather turned to strong drink and laudanum to numb his pain." A steely harshness rendered his tone clipped and cool. "He grew ever more bitter, unforgiving, and cruel, eventually taking his own life. As often happens when subjected to neglect and unkindness, my father was also given to drink and abuse."

Had Maxwell been mistreated by his father? Is that what he was saying? Did he realize his actions were not so very different than his sire's and grandsire's? A soft cry escaped her. "I…"

"Please, hear me out." His jaw tense, the duke held up a palm. A faint scar marred the flesh from forefinger to thumb.

Unprepared for the sympathy engulfing her, Gabriella swallowed and folded her hands in her lap. She clenched her fingers so tightly, the tips tingled.

He lied. That was all there was to it. He couldn't be telling the truth. He'd concocted this fanciful tale to steal Hartfordshire Court. Naturally, a wealthy duke's word would be believed over a humble land owner.

Her gentle Grandpapa was not capable of this sort of subterfuge. This evilness. This vileness. He simply wasn't.

Was he?

Tears stung her eyes, and she allowed the lids to drift shut as she battled to subdue her shock and grief. She would not give the duke the satisfaction of seeing her defeated and weeping.

"I only learned of this…your grandfather's part, last December," he continued softly. Again, a hint of regret or compassion made his voice rough. "Since then, I've been determined to return Hartfordshire Court to its rightful owners. Although my grandfather signed the deed of sale, the property was never legally transferred." He scrubbed a hand over his jaw. "The duchy has continued to pay the land and window taxes. I've spoken to my steward about that oversight, and he said the previous steward had always paid them, so he assumed he should continue to as well."

"It's not true," Gabriella breathed, barely recognizing her own raggedy, fragile voice. She swallowed again. “It cannot possibly be true.” She sounded like a well-trained parrot. But, a person didn’t live with someone for fifteen years and not know their character. Grandpapa was not a charlatan.

She wasn’t ready to admit defeat yet. What proof could Maxwell have?

“Yes, Gabriella, it is. I swear, every word.”

Such gentleness, and yes, even sympathy tempered his words, that tears welled again. Far easier for her to bear if he’d been all haughty, cold, accusing arrogance. *Oh God.* She held herself tightly, rocking forward and back. She didn’t want to believe a single word, but it explained so much over the years.

Why her grandfather rarely left Hartfordshire Court. Why he hadn’t any friends to speak of. Why Grandpapa held such animosity toward Maxwell.

“What…?” Bile, bitter and hot burned her throat. To have to even ask meant he knew she had doubts. She swallowed and forced the words out. “What proof have you?”

Maxwell took her hand, the action natural and comforting. A loyal granddaughter would’ve jerked free, railed at him, and rained curses down upon his handsome head. Yet she didn't.

Never before had she felt so fragile, that she might shatter with her next breath. Her whole world crumbled around her, and she was powerless to stop the destruction. To prevent the inevitable devastation this would wreak upon the people she most loved. Gabriella refused to berate herself for her momentary weakness. She was strong, but anyone who'd been dealt such a blow would need time to recover.

"I found my grandfather's journal in a hidden desk drawer. An entry revealed there'd been a card game with marked cards." The duke spoke slowly, his voice neutral, much like a barrister presenting a case before judges. "The entry also included the names of two other men involved. Herman Wakefield died a number of years ago, but my man of business was able to locate Wilson, Baronet Garrison. I've personally spoken with him, and he's provided a sworn statement. As young bucks up from university, a trifle disguised and short on funds, they agreed to vow my grandfather marked the cards in exchange for a few pounds apiece."

Gabriella pinched her lips together. "How do you know this Garrison person is telling the truth, Maxwell?" It occurred to her she'd slipped into using his given name with unnerving ease.

Even if he was lying, why would his grandfather have made such an entry if it weren't true? By their very nature, that was what journals were. A place to share all the secrets one couldn't reveal to the world.

Only the merest movement of his eyes indicated he'd heard her use of his given name. "What reason would he have to do so after all of these years?" He still held her hand. "No, Garrison's sickly and not long for this world. He said he wanted to right a wrong, and swears he had no idea your grandfather later blackmailed my grandfather and obtained Hartfordshire Court as a result."

She pulled her hand free, needing to cover her face and hide the stubborn tears seeping from her eyes. This couldn't be happening. It was impossible. Her grandfather couldn't be that kind of a scoundrel. A cheat. For if he was, then everything she'd known for the past fifteen years was a lie, and the Penningtons were indeed entitled to Hartfordshire Court.

Gabriella had never considered Maxwell might have a legitimate reason for his actions. She'd behaved abominably toward him, and he'd always remained a gentleman. Profound remorse and chagrin turned her cheeks hot.

Did Grandmama know of her husband's duplicity? Is that why she seldom ventured from Hartfordshire either? Had their dishonesty made them prisoners in the very house they'd stolen?

Listen to yourself. Have you so little faith in the people who've cared for you for over fifteen years? Can you so easily put aside your trust? Surely there's a logical explanation.

Lifting her face, she stared at the wildly rushing river. She appreciated how that tumultuous water felt. Tumbling over itself, bashed against the banks and the stones. Having no control over where it went, pushed and pulled along pell-mell.

A silent sigh whispered past her lips just as a crisp, white handkerchief appeared in her line of vision. "Here, *chèrie.*"

"I'm sure you understand that I should like to see the journal and Garrison's statement," she said softly. Guilt riddled her at even speaking the words.

"That can be arranged." No victory or triumph colored his voice. "I plan on presenting them to your grandfather in any event."

After drying her face, she folded his handkerchief and clutching it in one hand, studied her lap. "Why did you tell me this? I'm quite certain there's nothing I can do to prevent you from continuing along the path you've already started." A path he had a right to pursue if what he said was true. She raised her gaze and canted her head, straining to read his indecipherable features. "You spoke of ruin last night."

After wedging his hat and gloves between his thigh and the carriage side, he cupped her cheek. Rather than pulling away as she ought to do, as a woman presented with devastating information about the man who'd raised her was obliged to do, she closed her eyes instead.

And then she was in Maxwell's strong arms, his

warm, firm lips kissing her forehead, her eyes, her nose and finally, settling wondrously upon her mouth and tasting of coffee.

The world went silent. Utterly and completely. For certain the river still tumbled along, birds sang in the treetops, and the wind brushed her fingers through the verdant leaves and branches, but Gabriella heard them not. A coach and four might have passed on the road or thunder pealed through the heavens and she'd have heard neither.

And how did she respond to the passionate play upon her lips, the miserable, traitorous wretch that she was?

She looped her arms around his sturdy neck and kissed him back. Kissed him like a drowning woman gasping for air. Kissed him, as if this was the very last day she had to live, and everything she'd kept hidden, had denied even to herself, she could at last reveal, because nothing mattered anymore. And if in the midst of this horror, this nightmare, the imploding of her life, she could seize one tiny particle of happiness then by God, she'd do so.

I deserve it.

Even if Maxwell was the man about to wreak hell itself on her family and destroy everything Ophelia and Gabriella had ever known?

That sobering thought finally brought her to her senses, plunging her back to the awful present, and she jerked away, regret replacing her passion. "Your Grace…"

His breathing raspy, as if he struggled every bit as much as she to bring herself under control, he swiped the tears from her cheeks with his thumbs. Tears she wasn't even aware leaked from her eyes once more.

"Since I aim to marry you, *chérie*, you might as well continue to address me as Maxwell."

10

Whatever reaction Max had expected Gabriella to have, this wasn't it. She laughed. Not a dainty feminine tinkle, but a full on bent over at the waist, gasping for breath, belly laugh. His lips quirked of their own accord at her jubilant chuckles. He'd never seen her unfettered mirth and it was glorious. The reason for it, not as much.

Her focus snapped upward, her eyes going wide as she slapped a hand over her mouth. Her shoulders continued to shake, and the moisture pooling in her eyes now the color of turbulent clouds, was humor-induced. Beneath the straw bonnet shading her face, her beautiful gaze rounded impossibly more with realization.

"You're not serious?" Sobering, she knuckled away the moisture at the corner of her eyes. She leaned away, working her attention over him twice. "Stars above. You *are.* Are you utterly mad?"

Yes, he probably was.

Rather put a man off having his proposal laughed at, but then again, he hadn't exactly proposed in the most romantic way. Nothing about this was meant to be romantic. In fact, he wouldn't call it a marriage proposal at all, but rather bartering terms. She didn't know that yet, however.

Nonetheless, he knew her well enough to realize she wouldn't be pleased at what he said next. Would that he could go back six months, when he first recognized his feelings for Gabriella were more than admiration and attraction. Before he found his grandfather's diary, and Max started them upon this irreversible course.

While he had no doubt she would eventually agree to become his duchess, might even enjoy the physical aspect of their joining, he never believed she'd come to hold him in any regard. Especially after she learned of his terms.

What did that matter?

Most peers married for convenience. For power, position, coin. In this, he wasn't so very different, except that he meant to reclaim that which had been stolen from his family.

Damn his eyes, but a part of him wished it wasn't the reason.

She sat silent, her head slightly angled and her keen gaze still roving his face. Her attention lingered on his lips before flitting away. Was she remembering what had transpired between them but a few minutes ago?

Gabriella was attracted to him. The smoldering kisses they'd shared left no doubt.

He didn't dare ask for more. Didn't deserve more.

He'd chosen this path, perhaps not knowing all the consequences, but fully aware of what he must do. For justice, for righteousness and fairness. To avenge his grandmother, grandfather, and the child—the aunt or uncle he'd never known. And perhaps, part of this was revenge for himself as well.

His grandfather's inability to show kindness or love to his son had made Bronson a victim as well. And Bronson, a stranger to affection, had never learned how to love anyone, let alone his only child. Max had never experienced the love of a parent. Or a grandparent's. Or a sister's or brother's.

For all of his many friends at *Bon Chance*, some he considered as close as brothers and for whom he'd willingly die, no one in the entirety of his life, had ever said they loved *him*. He'd never heard the words, "I love you," directed to him.

He gave a little shake of his head, dispelling his self-pitying musings. This wasn't about him. *Isn't it?*

Perchance, he wasn't so very different than his sire or grandsire, after all. He hadn't expected his duchess would love him any more than he'd ever anticipated being struck by Cupid's arrow. *Ah, but Grandfather had loved Grandmother. And look where that landed him?* Too late for sentiment now, in any event. The die was cast, and there was naught to do but for Max to collect his winnings, no matter how acrimoniously acquired. *What's done is done.*

What an absurd time for Shakespeare to intrude upon his thoughts.

Gabriella had at last brought her chuckling under control, and as she continued to do at every turn, she surprised him once more. Rather than resort to histrionics or become a watering pot, she squared her shoulders and jutted that pert chin upward. "Your Grace—"

"Maxwell or Max, which is what I prefer. Unless you wish to address me as Pennington," he corrected quietly. "But even after seven years, whenever I hear the title, I still expect to glance over my shoulder and see my grandfather standing there."

Her eyebrows shied high on her smooth forehead. In that, she must've decided to concede. To mollify him or simply because it was easier?

"Maxwell, you may have the means to reclaim Hartfordshire Court, and though I'm loath to admit it, I do suspect what you're telling me is, at least, partially true. Nonetheless, I'm certain you can appreciate how devastating this news is. However, and regardless of the outcome, no way exists which will compel me to marry you." She skewed her mouth and crinkled her nose in the adorable way she did when confused or vexed. At least her toes weren't pattering away. *Yet.* "Besides, I fail to understand how one has anything whatsoever to do with the other."

Leaning back, he threaded his fingers together behind his head. This was where she would kick up a dust. Where he could expect recriminations, accusations, and protestations. No displays of emotions would make a jot of difference.

The sun's warmth felt glorious, and despite the impossibility of the situation, he relaxed, almost sliding into a drowsy doze. He hadn't slept last night. Truth be told, he hadn't slept much since deciding on this course of action. Because, despite being an utter arse for what he was about to do, he meant to proceed. His conscience and self-recriminations be damned.

"Maxwell, I need to return ho—that is to Hartfordshire Court." As she spoke, a bold bird landed atop Aphrodite's back and cocking its head, stared at them with curious little ebony eyes. A small smile quirked Gabriella's mouth as she whispered, "Hello there."

The bird took to wing as Max observed her through half-open eyes. "Already decided Hartfordshire isn't home any longer, have you?" He'd never been particularly fond of his childhood home, yet her distress was tangible and regret speared him.

A stricken expression chased her smile away, and angst whisked across her lovely face then was gone. He couldn't help but admire her ability to swiftly compose herself, and neither could he prevent the remorse gripping him that he'd caused her distress.

"Over an hour has passed, and they'll be expecting me," she quietly reminded him.

Gabriella Breckensole had pluck and resilience. She'd accepted the situation and attempted to make the best of it.

"I intend to speak to my grandfather about this matter as soon as I return home, Maxwell. I'm still not convinced your tale is true or accurate."

Her straightforwardness didn't surprise him. Did she truly believe Breckensole, who'd built his entire life on a series of lies, her life and Ophelia's as well, would tell the truth?

Straightening, Max dropped his foot to the coach floor. Hard. "I intend the same thing. But before we go, please listen to my proposal."

Her arched eyebrows crumpled together, and she brushed away an insect that had landed on her pale pink gown. "Is that a marriage proposal or another sort of proposal? For surely, you cannot believe I would marry you after this. Besides, I'm certain you wish a more noble duchess than the granddaughter of a clergyman's disgraced son."

That she could make a quip, given what she'd just learned, impressed him.

Max clenched his jaw and curled his toes in his too-damn tight boots, going over the speech he'd rehearsed so many times in his mind. Speaking the words aloud though, wasn't as easy as he'd anticipated. Saying them made everything all too real. Cruel and heartless.

"Gabriella." He chose to focus on the burbling water rather than her pale face with those too-big accusing eyes. "I intend to tell your grandfather that he, your grandmother, and your sister may continue to reside at Hartfordshire Court—"

"You would do that?" she gasped, clasping his forearm. "Even with what you know?" Wonder filled her voice.

"Don't become too excited or raise your hopes, *chérie*." He cut her a short glance.

She dropped her hand back into her lap, her mouth pursed and hazel gaze accusing.

He focused on a large boulder dividing the river. Far easier to do than witness her reaction. Her disappointment and disillusionment. Perhaps, even her hatred. *When did I become a coward too*?

At the moment, he didn't much like himself and doubted he'd ever do so again.

"I shall insist upon your grandfather offering Hartfordshire Court as your dowry. Through our children, the estate will revert to my family as it should." The idea of this woman carrying his child speared a burst of lust so strong, he had to swallow and shift his position before continuing. "Until such time she weds, Ophelia may either reside with your grandparents or live with us. I shall also permit your grandparents to remain at Hartfordshire until their deaths."

His man of business had done his research. Harold Breckensole had no legal heirs, save Gabriella and her twin. The estate would've passed to them had it been properly transferred.

Gabriella slumped into her seat, disbelief wreathing her face.

"By taking these measures, my family will regain Hartfordshire Court, but your grandparents, and thereby you, and your sister, will be spared the scandal that will ensue if I have to make your grandfather's cheating, blackmail, and tax fraud public. Furthermore, since the duchy has paid Hartfordshire's taxes all these years and the estate is still registered in my family's name, this is the wisest recourse." He pulled on his gloves, giving her time to digest what she'd just heard.

Putting two fingers to her temple, she rubbed them in a circular motion and began tapping her toes in that familiar cadence. "Can't you simply have a written agreement with my grandfather that upon his and my grandmother's deaths, the property reverts back to you? Or is that even necessary?" She scrunched her nose. "According to you, the deed was never transferred. Could we not just pay rents?"

Yes, he could permit Breckensole to remain and let Hartfordshire Court, but he doubted the man had the funds. The matter of the back taxes must be addressed as well. There was no way on God's green earth Breckensole hadn't known he wasn't paying his taxes. The blasted deed of sale was also an issue.

Max's solicitor had warned if they went to court over the matter, there was a small—very small—chance the document might be enforceable. As if things weren't complicated enough, even if it turned out Breckensole legally owned Hartfordshire Court despite the manner in which he'd gained the estate, he owed decades of taxes plus interest to the duchy.

Funds, Max knew full well, Breckensole didn't have and had absolutely no hope of acquiring. In essence, the taxes were a lien upon the estate. And what was more on point, he wasn't feeling at all charitable. He wanted Breckensole to suffer. Wanted him to suffer the way his grandfather and grandmother had suffered. The way his father had suffered.

The way *he* had suffered.

What he didn't want, damn his eyes, was for Gabriella to suffer too. The only way that wouldn't happen is if he was a bloody magnanimous saint and forgave the whole debacle. Resentment welled, and his gut cramped. That he couldn't do. Wouldn't do.

Breckensole didn't deserve the reprieve.

"Couldn't we, please?" she all but pleaded, placing her small hand on his forearm again.

Max understood what it took this regal woman to put aside her pride and utter those words. To beg. She didn't grovel for herself, but for her family, as he'd known she would. Her sacrifice heaped more coals upon his already guilty conscience.

He shook his head before donning his hat. "It's not possible. My desire is to avoid gossip and a scandal. There's been enough of that in recent years, tarnishing the dukedom."

Damn my duchy and my family's reputation. Some

things, Gabriella and her wishes, are more important than my bloody good name and repute.

So expressive were her eyes, he could practically read her thoughts tripping about in her mind. "I've already had my solicitor draw up an agreement," he advised without looking in her direction again, for his resolve wavered. "I also have a special license. And as soon as the contract is signed between your grandfather and me, you and I shall be married. *If* that's the route you decide you want to take." Bringing his attention back to her, he ran his gaze over her face.

Ire flared in her bright eyes and color flushed her cheeks.

God, she was absolutely glorious when riled.

"This is more about revenge and retribution than it is about restoring Hartfordshire Court to your family." She jabbed a finger at his chest. "You've taken up someone else's offense as your own, and while part of me understands your anger, the solution you've arrived at is ludicrous."

"Gabby—"

Making a curt gesture with her hand, she scowled.

"Have you truly convinced yourself that by forcing me to marry you, you're being benevolent? Everything you've suggested can be done without us resorting to nuptials. It seems you intend to be as cruel as your father and grandfather," she scoffed. "The apple doesn't fall far from the tree, does it?"

Her accusation stinging, he leveled her a thunderous scowl. Wasn't she taking up her grandfather's cause? But there was a tangible difference. She protected the living, whilst he wanted to exonerate the dead.

She gave a short, caustic, entirely humorless laugh, the harsh sound lancing his soul. "And to think, more fool me, at one time I believed myself enamored of you."

The fool doth think he is wise, but the wise man knows himself to be a fool.

More ill-timed Shakespearian wisdom?

The next thing he knew, he'd start recalling Bible verses, which would, in truth, not be so very astonishing as one of his overly zealous tutor, Mr. Fogart, had made Max write verses for the merest infraction. For instance, substituting molasses for ink or flavoring the lemonade with vinegar. He'd been made to write, "The student is not above the teacher" from Luke, no less than five hundred times for placing ants in the man's bed.

At one time, I believed myself enamored of you.

Of all the things she just said, the truth, she'd unhesitatingly hurled at him, that bit was what reverberated in his mind. It stirred what he heartily hoped was not doubt or misgivings at this late juncture.

Arms folded in a defensive posture, she tilted her head. The breeze caught the pink ribbons of her bonnet and sent them fluttering. "Tell me, Maxwell. Why me and not Ophelia?"

"I think, *chérie,* you already know the answer to that."

"Stop calling me that," she snapped, giving his shoulder a hard punch. "And I do *not* know the answer, else I wouldn't have asked. Please do enlighten me. I cannot wait to hear what rubbish you concoct." She really was a tart-mouthed minx. Most excellent. Such fortitude would be useful and sustain her going forward.

"There's been a powerful attraction between us since we first met, Gabriella. Tell me it doesn't call to you as it does me."

She snorted, loudly and indelicately. "Ballocks, you vain popinjay."

Max checked a delighted chuckle. She'd truly kick up a fuss if he dared laugh at her frustration.

"God knows, I've tried to fight it, resist the draw." He drummed long square-tipped fingers atop his thigh. "Especially when I learned of your grandfather's treachery." Shrugging again, he gathered the reins. "I know you won't believe this, and I don't expect you to, but I rather think we would march along well. I had intended to call upon your grandfather to ask if I might pay my addresses before this ugliness came to light."

Not that old Breckensole would've consented with the history Max now knew existed between the families.

For once at a loss for words, she simply stared. Inhaling a ragged breath, she touched the shoulder she'd just clobbered. A thrill bolted through him. Even now, when he was at his worst, when he'd delivered such ugly information to her, the merest touch sent his lust soaring.

"Maxwell, you don't have to do this. I'm sure we can come to another solution." Looking lost, she glanced around, blinking almost as if surprised to see where she was. "My family can… we can move. Go somewhere else."

No. I don't want you to leave.

He'd considered that option for all of one second before dismissing the idea. It wouldn't deliver the outcome he desired. "Where? And live on what? You have no source of income. Do you have relatives you might impose upon?"

"No."

The single syllable said much. The Breckensoles had nowhere to turn. No place to go. No one to take them in. He made an I-suspected-as-much-sound in the back of his throat.

"The way I see it, there are three options." He lifted his forefinger. "I take your grandfather to court for fraud, blackmail, and tax evasion. He'll spend the remainder of his life in prison, and you, your sister, and your ailing grandmother would be left to deal with the ensuing disgrace and would end up on the street."

She notched her chin upward, clearly not the least impressed with her first choice. "The other options?"

He held up a second finger. "Your grandfather agrees to destroy the deed of sale, pays monthly rents, and repays the taxes that the dukedom has paid on his behalf for decades. Mind you, we're talking thousands of pounds." He steeled his facial features and his emotions against her tiny, distressed gasp. "We both know he doesn't have those kinds of funds nor can he lay his hands on them."

No friends or family stood in the eaves ready to lend him a hand, a factor that played to Max's advantage.

He raised his ring finger. "Or three—"

"I marry you," she said very softly, her voice a mere whisper. "And my grandfather dowers me with Hartfordshire Court. Which, you must own, is just plain stupid since you claim the estate belongs to you anyway."

"It saves a great deal of complication and public scandal, which I'd prefer to avoid," he said. "I can only presume you would as well for yourself and your family's sake."

The silence lengthened, stretching out before them, tense and uncompromising. Finally, she released a wispy sigh. "You'll allow my family to live at Hartfordshire without paying rents? No taxes due? No possibility of eviction?" She flicked three of her fingers up.

Then a fourth levered upward

The little vixen. Had to outdo him, didn't she?

"And my grandfather continues grazing his cattle on the property without any fee or a partial commission to you when they are sold? And…"

Her thumb sprang up.

Five bloody conditions? Damn, but he'd underestimated her negotiating skills.

Her chin notched skyward another inch. "You'll also provide Ophelia a ten-thousand-pound dowry."

Astonishment jerked Max's head up, but after a moment of staring into her wounded gaze, nearly drowning in the fathomless depths, he gave a terse nod.

She'd added terms he hadn't considered and not a single request had been for herself.

Nonetheless, he had no qualms with her provisions. If it brought her peace of mind and helped her to feel like she had a measure of control, so be it.

"As you very well know, you could grant every one of those conditions now if you wished to. Not the dowry for Ophelia of course, but all of the rest." Though her face was alabaster pale, she met his gaze unflinchingly.

By God, she was brave. A remarkable woman, indeed.

"I could. But Harold Breckensole doesn't deserve that kind of grace or forgiveness. And knowing one of his beloved granddaughters had to sacrifice herself, because of his selfishness, will eat away at him for the rest of his days." He couldn't prevent the rancor edging each clipped word.

Just as losing Grandmother had gnawed at Grandfather.

"You are a cruel man, Maxwell." Something akin

to profound disappointment along with resignation and no small amount of resentment shone in Gabriella's eyes. "You would do well to remember, that someday, you will stand before God, and you'll be judged as harshly as you have judged others. You'd best pray the day never comes that *you* need forgiveness."

Too late.

Max flexed his jaw. Yes, he was cruel. He'd learned about cruelty firsthand. As for the other? Well, wasn't it true that those who'd committed wrongs were usually the first to demand forgiveness and often quoted scripture to enhance their manipulation? He suspected though, he might very well end up as miserable as his sire and grandsire.

"Which is it to be, Gabriella?" Hands on the reins, he spared her a short glance from the side of his eye. "The choice is yours."

"No, it's not. It's never been mine." She gave a fragile, broken laugh. "I shall grow to hate you. You know that, don't you? Anything that may have turned into warmth or affection, any desire I may now have for you, bitterness and resentment will eventually corrode into loathing. If you insist upon this path, are you prepared for a life every bit as miserable as that of your father's and your grandfather's?"

"I know what I'm doing," he bit out, not at all pleased to have his thoughts read and vocalized.

She pressed on, relentless in *her* judgment. "You're making me pay the penalty for a crime that wasn't mine. My only sin is being Harold Breckensole's granddaughter. Something I have no control over whatsoever. You, however, do have a choice whether you choose to forgive or carry a grudge. I'm not saying you and yours weren't wronged, or that if my grandfather is guilty, there shouldn't be recompense, but this…"

"It is what a duke would do. What he does for his duchy and family," Max ground out.

She flicked a hand between them. "I vow you will come to regret it, and if this is what a duke would do, then I am very much glad I was born a commoner."

They'd reached the road, and the gig jostled her against him as the vehicle crested the low embankment. They rode in strained silence until the bridge came into view, and Max slowed Aphrodite once more. He turned to look straight into Gabriella's eyes, the anguish there, the accusation and condemnation, stabbing him to his core like a rusty two-sided sword.

Yet, it wasn't enough to put aside the vengeance that had burned inside him for months. How could he just let it go? Forgive the offense? The treachery? A better man might be able to, but then again, he'd never claimed to be a good man. Dutiful, loyal, well-mannered, the epitome of *haut ton* refinement, honest, and on occasion given to mirth and benevolence.

But never good.

"What's it to be then, Gabriella?" He used the same tone he used to soothe a skittish horse. "Which of the three do you choose, because as you said the sin is not yours? So you will make this decision. Not me. Not your grandfather or your grandmother or your sister. You."

Snorting, she shook her head, her disgust palpable. "As if any of them have appeal." Her eyes drifted closed for a moment, and she released a ragged sigh, her cheeks puffing out slightly with the exhalation. "You've given me no alternative, and you well know that. Since I must pick, as you knew I would, I select the third option."

Max gave a curt nod, at once exalting in the small victory and also grieving for the wound he'd inflicted on this gentlewoman. She wasn't deserving of this. She was a pawn and he'd used her unforgivably for vengeance. This doublemindedness would likely drive him mad. He hopped to the ground and allowed himself a moment to bring his chaotic thoughts under control before striding to her side and lifting his arms to help her down.

She stared at his hands, indecision whisking across her refined features. He had no doubt she wanted to tell him to go to the devil—was actually surprised she already hadn't.

Still, they would be man and wife. And damn it all, he'd treat her with the dignity and respect a duchess deserved, because that's what a duke did, as he'd told her. A duke took care of his dukedom. His family. Of the people entrusted to his care. Of his lands, village, tenants, and servants, and God knew the Pennington Duchy had long, *long* been neglected.

Dukes don't destroy young women's hopes and futures.

At last, she permitted him to assist her from the conveyance. Head held high, and shoulders squared, she met his gaze directly. "I'll explain to my family what has occurred. You may come for dinner at seven."

He lifted his hat and canted his head in a brief bow. "I shall be there."

"But know this, Your Grace."

He didn't miss the deliberate cool politeness she'd reverted to.

"I shall never come to your bed willingly. *Never.* You'll have to force me each and every time we copulate if you want your heirs." A miserable smile pulled her soft mouth upward. "I wonder, in a decade or two, if you'll still think your revenge was worth it."

Hell, he was beginning to doubt it even now. Though he knew it was her anger speaking, he could no more violate his sweet Gabriella than pluck the sun from the sky or dam the ocean. Seduction, though… Her kisses told him, she desired him too. “Gabriella?” He touched her cheek, but she flinched away, her expression hard and gaze frosty.

“I’ll not succumb to your seductive wiles anymore, Duke.”

She meant it. The magical kisses they’d shared would be the only affection he’d ever receive from her. From anyone. She spun on her heel and took several strides before swinging back to face him, utter devastation ravaging her lovely features.

“I could have loved you, Maxwell,” she said on a sob before running down the drive.

Tears pricked his eyes.

I could have loved you too, my darling Gabby.

11

One glimpse of Gabriella's face when she returned from her outing with the Duke of Pennington, and Ophelia dragged her to her bedchamber. With a swift glance up and down the corridor, she closed the door then spun to face her twin, demanding an explanation.

"Gabby, whatever has happened? You were gone for nearly two hours, and you appear as if… Well… I'm not certain exactly what you look like except there is a haunted glint in your eyes that frightens me." Three neat lines appeared on her forehead, and she wrinkled her nose, staring pointedly at Gabriella's empty hands. "And where are your sketch pad and pencils?"

"Botheration." Gabriella groaned as she untied her bonnet wishing she might speak the foul oath on the tip of her tongue. "I left them in the duke's gig."

Ophelia stopped fussing with the fringe of the pillow she'd picked up and went poker stiff. "Perhaps you should explain from the beginning, because I believe I just heard you say, your drawing supplies were in the duke's gig. I presume you refer to the Duke of Pennington?"

Something in Gabriella's expression must've given her away for Ophelia tossed aside the pillow and said, "Yes, just as I presumed. But you told me you were going for a walk and to sketch, and you do not, in general, dissemble."

"I lied." No sense in prevaricating about it. She had, and from her sister's astonished expression, she'd deduced more was afoot. No one could ever mistake Ophelia for a bacon brain. "But I assure you, dearest, I had an exceptionally good reason for doing so."

Trying to save her family from utter ruin and a madman's vengeance. She'd failed. No, not entirely, she hadn't. She'd protected her family, but at a cost most dear.

Gabriella dumped the bonnet on her dressing table, avoiding glancing in the mirror as she reached to unfasten her spencer. "How is your headache? Aren't you to leave for Jessica's soon?"

"My headache is gone, but dear Jessica has a megrim now," Ophelia said. "A note came while you were out. We've rescheduled for next week." Impatience fairly radiating off her, and arms akimbo, Ophelia drummed her fingertips on her hips. "What's this explanation for lying, for I've never known you to flat out fib before?"

More of the duke's unsavory influence.

Gabriella was aware turmoil roiled in her eyes and also that her lips might be the merest bit rosy from that extraordinary kiss. Hopefully, her sister would credit her countenance to the blustery weather.

After removing her spencer and gloves, she sank onto the mattress, completely drained. Not surprising since her life had just been toppled teapot handle over spout. Once she'd reconciled herself to what she must do, a peculiar sort of peace had enveloped her. Rather, a numbness that enabled her to function in a sort of hazy, incredulous cloud.

As succinctly as possible, she shared the dismal tale, somewhat amazed at her ability to do so without collapsing into a weeping blob of hysteria. She judiciously omitted the part about the scintillating kisses. Of everything that had occurred, this last kiss made the least sense. How could she have responded so wantonly? How could she have permitted a knave of his caliber such liberties?

Not fair, her conscience scolded. She couldn't place all the blame for that intimate interlude on his shoulders. Not when their previous kisses had made her eager—hungry—for his embrace. She'd enjoyed the experience far too much, and as furious as she presently was with him, feared her declaration about sharing a bed might've been incensed bluster. She'd all but melted into his arms with little provocation.

True, but that was before he'd shown his hand, and she'd seen what an immoral lout he truly was. She mightn't have any control over these circumstances, but she could withhold her affection and passion. “So, you see, Fee Fee, there’s naught else to be done but for me to wed the duke.”

Her twin’s jaw dropped open, and her hazel eyes so like Gabriella’s rounded in incredulity before the irises almost disappeared as she narrowed her eyes into wrathful slits.

“Oh, my God. Oh, my *God!* The churl. The fiend. The…the…reprehensible, scapegracing bastard.” Ophelia’s voice jumped an octave on the last word, and she, too, plopped unceremoniously onto the bed. “Gabby, you cannot—*simply cannot*!—marry Pennington under these wretched circumstances. Why, it amounts to nothing short of extortion.”

It did indeed. And in Gabriella’s mind, that made Maxwell no better than Grandpapa. Worse, for she held no affection for the duke. *Keep telling yourself that and perchance you’ll come to believe it.* Teeth clamped until they ached, she squashed the intrusive thought. She wasn’t one to mistake feminine lust and curiosity for something more meaningful.

She grabbed another floral pillow and plunking

the soft square on her lap, plucked at the silky gold fringe. "There isn't any alternative. If Grandpapa is guilty, and I fear he very well might be, I cannot allow him to go to prison for the rest of his life. He's old and frail and would die within months.

"Nor would I ever consider permitting you and Grandmama to be put out of your home. I suppose we ought to appreciate the duke allowing me any choice at all. He might've booted us to the curb and seized all without consideration."

All outraged sisterly protector, Ophelia snuffled loudly and scrubbed at her damp cheeks. "And here I believed Pennington a decent, chivalrous sort. I even suspected you held a *tendre* for him. I would never have believed him capable of such vileness. Oh, my darling sister, I cannot bear it. I simply cannot comprehend that you would even consider making such a sacrifice." She punched her pillow. "God rot the blackguard. If I were a man, I'd call him out."

Now there was a lovely thought. A duel at dawn. Fisticuffs at four? Swords at six? Sabers at seven? Gabriella snorted at her own absurdity.

What would the pompous, self-righteous Duke of Pennington do if she challenged him to an affair of honor? Had such a thing ever been done? A woman demanding satisfaction? Not with a man, though there were a few isolated instances of women dueling other women.

He wouldn't accept of course. A duke most certainly wouldn't concede to duel with a woman. And most definitely not a lady very nearly his affianced. Oh, what a succulent treat that would be for the gossip rags. What that wouldn't do to his efforts to keep everything hush-hush.

Mayhap she'd pen a letter or two *or ten* to the most notorious of the tattle magazines.

No, she wouldn't. Because it wasn't only his name and reputation that would be dragged through the filth. She stopped fiddling with the fringe and shot a frantic glance to her bedchamber door.

Dear God, Grandpapa wouldn't do something so rash as to demand satisfaction, would he? Did he even own a blunderbuss or a blade of any sort except for kitchen and garden utensils?

Flopping onto her back, she stared at the familiar, pleated fern-green canopy. “The duke is coming to dinner at seven tonight. I must talk to our grandparents beforehand. It will be horridly awkward when he arrives.” She turned her head, reaching for her sister’s hand. “He wants us wed straightaway, as if he almost fears Grandpapa will contrive a way to save Hartfordshire Court. Though, I confess, if all that Pennington said is true, I cannot conceive it.”

“Neither can I,” Ophelia whispered, her voice breaking. “This is awful beyond belief.”

Biting her lower lip, Gabriella closed her eyes for a blink. “Maxwell is ruthless and unforgiving, Fee Fee. He cannot be reasoned with. God knows I tried. I really, truly tried.”

And he was absolutely undeterred in his quest for retribution.

“No. It’s unthinkable. You cannot bind yourself to such a monster.” Ophelia thumped the mattress with her fist. “Grandpapa shan’t permit it. You’ll see. There must be an alternative.”

“I’m of age now,” Gabriella reminded her quietly.

"The decision is mine to make."

Her twin shook her head vehemently. Several pins came loose, and tendrils of hair tumbled to her shoulders. She put a shaky palm to her forehead. "I fear what the shock will do to our grandparents."

Gabriella's exact concern.

Swallowing, she dipped her chin in a nod. "I've the same worry, and that's why my mind is made up. Trust me when I tell you, Pennington has thought of everything. He provided me with three options, and I've selected the least dire. This way, I am assured you and our grandparents won't suffer from his wrath. You'll still have a home, and the duke is willing to cancel the tax debt grandpapa owes the duchy. In truth," she gave a raspy, unhappy chuckle, "I suppose there is a degree of benevolence in this particular solution."

She doubted the verity of the words even as she murmured them.

Ophelia snorted and launched the pillow across the room. "Ballocks. He's a selfish blackguard for reclaiming Hartfordshire Court and entrapping you. I'll bet my best bonnet, you're what he's been after all along."

Even if nothing was further from the truth, Gabriella adored her sister for the suggestion.

"The knave knew you were beyond him," Ophelia insisted, torturing the poor coverlet with her nails. "That he was undeserving of someone as wonderful as you, so he resorted to nefarious means to claim your hand."

Genuine amusement caused Gabriella's burst of laughter. "Oh, Fee Fee, come now. The duke can have his pick of any number of women. A penniless commoner most assuredly does not top his list of eligible ladies. Rest assured, I never set my cap for him, and there's no danger of a broken heart."

He'd already shattered the organ to fragments. She doubted she'd be capable of feeling anything romantic for a very long time.

If ever again.

"Hmph." Arms crossed, Ophelia glared moodily at the canopy. "Our maternal great-grandfather was an Italian count. That ought to amount to something. And

I don't believe you when you say, you've no interest in Pennington. I'm your twin, remember. I *know* you. You did entertain warm feelings for him."

"I'll warrant, I found him charming when we returned from finishing school." Intriguing and exciting too. "I was also struck by his good looks and humor, and prior to learning he intended to take Hartfordshire Court from us, I may have engaged in silly schoolgirl notions. But that's all they were. In any event, I have since discovered that a handsome face can hide a blackguard's heart."

As she spoke the words, Gabriella knew them to be false. But if the untruth eased Ophelia's worry a jot, she'd keep vowing to feeling nothing for Maxwell but enmity.

I could have loved you. Those words replayed in her mind, a relentless mantra of what would never be. She could have loved him. Might've been well on the way to doing so. But not now. She wouldn't permit the tender emotion to grow and bloom. Not when he forced her into a union.

He'd have his duchess, all right. A frigid,

hardhearted harridan of his creation brought about by the reprisal he demanded. She'd make sure he was as miserable as she, and there'd be no more willing kisses or anything else. Perchance, she'd stipulate they didn't reside in the same house.

Mouth pursed, she blew out a wobbly sigh before sitting up. Not only would she hate Maxwell, in time, she feared she'd come to despise herself too. For it wasn't her nature to be vindictive and unforgiving.

She peered over her shoulder at her twin.

Ophelia sat up, but her face remained twisted in indignation as she worried her lower lip.

"Will you come with me to talk to Grandmama and Grandpapa? I don't think I can approach them with these ugly allegations alone." Cowardliness was foreign to Gabriella. Nonetheless, assertions such as these…Well, they weren't easy accusations to make. "I feel an absolute traitor," she confided. "I know beyond a doubt, it will break their hearts, and neither is as strong as they once were."

At once, Ophelia pulled her into a fierce embrace. "Of course, dearest. Of course I shall. You may think there's no other recourse but for you to marry Pennington, but I'm not ready to quit the field quite yet. Perhaps Grandpapa has an explanation or a remedy. Mayhap there's a way out of this conundrum that you haven't thought of."

"Such as?" There was no way out.

Waggling her winged eyebrows, Ophelia gave a wicked wink. "What about poison in his wine? Loosening his saddle's girth? A fall down the stairs?"

"Shall I bring the shovel, or will you?" Permitting a rueful smile, Gabriella gathered her scattered thoughts and emotions. "Let me freshen up, and we'll go below. Pray to God the shock doesn't overwhelm our grandparents."

12

Fifteen minutes later, Gabriella had settled comfortably in the parlor, her favorite room at Hartfordshire Court. The sun shone through a beveled-leaded glass window, adorning the chamber in a myriad of miniature rainbows. A hearty fire snapped and popped in the hearth framed by a carved mahogany mantel. The outdated furnishings, intended for comfort rather than to impress, gave the chamber a welcoming ambiance.

As she curled her legs beneath her in her usual corner of the blue and gold-striped brocade sofa opposite the fireplace, she examined the room with a fresh eye.

She'd read dozens, probably hundreds, of books in this very spot. Birthdays and Christmastide had been celebrated here as well. She still remembered being a frightened five-year-old and her grandmother's soft arms embracing her as she whispered soothing, reassuring words in her ear despite her own grief at having lost her son and daughter-in-law so tragically.

Now Gabriella's newfound knowledge tainted the comforting room. Had the house been furnished when Grandpapa acquired the estate? If not, where had the funds to purchase the furnishings and everything else in the house come from? What about the monies to send her and Ophelia to school? To buy their clothing? Did the sale of the cattle truly provide enough capital to live on?

Were there more dark secrets yet to be revealed?

So much doubt plagued her when once there'd been absolute trust. She wanted to shout at the unfairness, but histrionics and emotional outbursts served no purpose. She'd seen the unyielding granite hardness of Maxwell's jaw. Recognized the flinty ruthlessness in his steely gaze. He was a man bent on vengeance.

Come hell or highwater.

That was what he'd vowed months ago, and he'd kept his word.

True, it was beyond her comprehension to understand the kind of hatred and animosity that motivated a man to go to the extremes for revenge that he had. But she had been raised in a loving home with caring grandparents, whereas he'd never known kindness or affection. While it was true her grandfather was reluctant to part with his coin, she and her sister had never lacked for essentials, including love.

Sorrow pinched her heart, and she blinked away the sting of hot tears. Had this life been based on a lie? Was all of this, she glanced around the cozy room once more, a lie too?

Despite the robust fire, a shiver skittered down her spine. Just how soon did Maxwell expect the wedding ceremony to take place? Three months ago, she would've been over the moon to think she'd gained the attention of a much-sought after gentleman. A man who'd captivated her since their first meeting.

He'd been right about their mutual attraction, though she'd chew shoe leather rather than confess such idiocy to him. There had been something sparking and sizzling between them before he trampled it unmercifully on this path of retribution.

Bearing a tea tray, Ophelia entered, followed by their grandmother, looking much recovered from her bout of ill-health. Her silver-threaded hair twisted into a tidy knot at the back of her head, Grandmama wore her gray gown trimmed in burgundy braid today.

Once Ophelia placed the tray on the low tea table, she promptly set about pouring the fragrant brew. Ah, new tea leaves, and even two kinds of biscuits. A rare treat indeed.

Gabriella caught her sister's eye and sent her an appreciative smile.

A moment later, Grandpapa shuffled into the parlor. Purplish half-moon shadows darkened the skin below his eyes and weariness etched his beloved face, deepening the many craggy creases. Almost three and seventy, he'd aged much this past year. He'd lost weight too.

Did the secrets and guilt he bore haunt him? Rob him of sleep and peace and his appetite? Well, at least he'd be able to rest easier now, once the truth was aired. Secrets ate away at a person. Gabriella would've preferred to have this ugliness kept hidden, despite the cathartic effect of confessing.

"What's this?" He motioned toward the tea service, in the tiniest hint of disapproval at the extravagance. "New tea leaves and *two* types of biscuits," his taut eyebrows said.

"Shush, Harold," Grandmother admonished gently. "We didn't have a birthday celebration for the girls. I think they're deserving of an extra dainty."

He harrumphed but helped himself to a ginger biscuit. "You asked to speak to your grandmother and me, Gabriella?" Wearing the same faded walnut-brown suit he'd donned for years, he assumed his usual place in the parlor, the wingback chair angled slightly away from the fireplace and which afforded him the window light as well.

With an unexpectedly grateful smile, he accepted the cup Ophelia handed him. Once Grandmama had her tea and a Shrewsbury biscuit in hand, her sister picked a seat on the sofa beside Gabriella.

His bald pate shining from the fire's and the sunlight's reflection, Grandpapa quirked a wiry gray eyebrow. "Well, what has you both looking like you have a case of the blue devils? Did a beau fail to pay you proper attention last evening?" He straightened, his faded gaze flicking between the twins. "I say, did something untoward occur at the music party last evening?"

Gabriella hid a wince. He couldn't know.

Before she could answer, he turned his faded gaze on Grandmama. "We'd best send a chaperone along from now on, Irene." *Who? The maid of all work?* "We wouldn't want the chinwags targeting our girls."

Our girls. Yes, she and her sister had been their girls for these past fifteen years, and Gabriella hadn't a doubt what she was about to say would crush her grandparents. Either because they revealed the truth, or because she mistrusted them enough to put forth the harsh questions.

Summoning her resolve, she wrapped both hands

around the teacup, savoring the warmth. She hadn't realized how chilled she'd become. Could it be that bitterness had already begun to turn her heart cold? Could resentment truly do so that swiftly? A shiver tip-toed across her shoulders at the wretched thought.

God, what a miserable future she faced.

Yes, but my family will be secure.

With a boldness that astounded her, she lifted her head and peered squarely into her grandfather's eyes. "Grandpapa, the Duke of Pennington claims he has evidence that you cheated his grandfather at cards and blackmailed the sixth duke into selling you Hartfordshire Court." She rushed on before he could interrupt. "Pennington will join us for dinner at seven of the clock tonight. He's demanding you settle Hartfordshire on me as a dowry and that I marry him to keep the scandal quiet."

The shattering of china wrenched a gasp from Ophelia. "Grandmama!"

Gabriella's attention flew to her grandmother. Pale as death, Grandmama held a quaking hand over her mouth as she stared aghast at her husband of almost five-and-forty years.

"I told you it was too great a risk, Harold," she whispered hoarsely. "I *told* you."

His jaw stiff and eyebrows forming a harsh vee, Grandpapa set his teacup down. It rattled and clanked, sloshing tea over the rim into the saucer. Shoulders slumped, chin tucked to his chest, he covered his eyes with one gnarled hand.

It's true.

God above, was *everything* Maxwell claimed true?

By the reaction of her beloved grandparents, a great deal of what she'd suggested must be. Hands shaking, she set her teacup down too. More from a need to do something, she rose and after tossing a serviette upon the puddle of tea, gathered the broken china and set the pieces atop the table.

She mopped up the tea as best she could, the whole while a righteous anger she didn't know she could feel toward her grandparents burgeoned in her middle. The emotion welled ever higher and higher until she climbed to her feet and whispered accusingly, "How could you have done something so despicable?

Didn't you consider the long-term consequences?"

Tears sliding down her papery cheeks, Grandmama shook her head and fumbled for the handkerchief in her sleeve. "He did it for me. Everything was for me."

Struggling for control, Gabriella slowly sank upon the sofa's arm. "Grandpapa cheated at cards and blackmailed the sixth Duke of Pennington for you? I do not understand—"

"May he burn in hell," Grandpapa snarled. "I'd cheat him again, and I'd blackmail him again too. I'd do it over and over and over a thousand times for what that devil put Irene through." He pointed a shaking finger at his wife. "She was the duchess's companion, and that spawn of Satan forced himself upon her."

Gabriella felt every bit of color leave her face as a peculiar iciness and a wave of light-headedness engulfed her. She exchanged a horrified glance with her twin, and could see her own shock reflected in her sister's eyes. "Are you saying…?" Oh God, Gabriella could barely form the foul words. "That he took *liberties* with Grandmama, and that's why you cheated at cards and blackmailed him?"

"That's precisely what I'm saying." Bitterness dripping from each word, he slouched in his chair, looking old and defeated and feeble beyond description. "A peer always escapes justice for his crimes. Nevertheless, by God, I made certain that Benedict, the inglorious sixth Duke of Pennington paid a price."

"But," she blurted, scarcely able to comprehend what she'd heard. "He was married. In fact, that's one of the reasons the current duke is so angry. He claims his grandfather resorted to drink and laudanum after his wife died. He blames you for her death and that of their unborn child as well. Possibly the spare heir."

"Horseshit!" Grandpapa banged both fist upon the chair's arms, then slammed them down again. "That's utter horse. Shit."

The women gasped in unison. Grandpapa didn't curse in the presence of ladies.

"Pennington had a penchant for opium and drink long before I took advantage of his vices," he practically growled. "His poor wife died of a broken heart, because the bastard swived anything in skirts. Whether the woman was willing or not."

"Harold," Grandmama cautioned, her face and posture radiating her unease. "The girls…"

"Nay, I'll not temper my speech. Neither of the twins is a wilting flower." Grandpapa jabbed his thumb toward his wife. "Your grandmother wasn't the first, or the last woman he forced himself on. I've no doubt he raped the duchess too."

Surely Maxwell had no knowledge of this…ghastliness. Fighting the nausea swirling in her belly, Gabriella pressed her fingers between her eyes. "But the duke found his grandfather's journal. It speaks of two other men involved in the card game and how upset the duchess was when her familial home was lost."

Grandpapa sat back and folded his hands over his stomach. He nodded gravely but without a hint of remorse. "'Tis true Hartfordshire was the duchess's ancestral home. I have no compunction about admitting I wanted to inflict as much misery on Pennington as he'd caused your grandmother and me. I do regret the duchess's sorrow. She was a kind woman deserving of some happiness."

"Indeed, she was," Grandmama's soft voice intruded, her eyes slightly unfocused as she gazed blindly out the window to the charming, sundrenched flower garden. These memories obviously distressed her greatly. "You see, my darling girls, Harold and I were betrothed. And after Pennington…" She dragged in a juddery breath. "Well, after he defiled me," she dabbed at her eyes again, "I found myself with child."

"Dear God," Ophelia cried, hurrying to crouch before her grandmother's knees. "How awful it must've been for you all these years as that family is our nearest neighbors."

"Yes, indeed," Grandmama acknowledged. "Which is why we've stayed so close to home. After a few years of doing so, it became more comfortable than going out." She closed her eyes and rested her head against the back of her chair. "I knew it was wrong to allow your grandfather to seek vengeance on my behalf. But how I hated Pennington. *I* craved revenge."

Her eyelashes trembled before her eyelids swept open, and what Gabriella saw there scoured her soul. The deadness in her cherished grandmother's eyes nearly drew a sob from her.

"I was glad to do it, Irene. To teach him and those other toffs a lesson," Grandpapa said. "He deserved everything that happened to him. And more for all of the lives he callously ruined, just because he could."

Perhaps so, but did the rest of the sixth duke's family have to suffer the consequences too? Couldn't Grandpapa see that now she and her sister and even Grandmama were going to reap the cost, much as the duchess, Maxwell's father, and even Maxwell himself had?

Or did vengeance blind one to all else, make a person disregard everything, so keen was the drive to retaliate? That Maxwell and Grandpapa were capable of such behavior grieved her spirit. In the wake of the visceral emotions, the air had become thick and cloying, the simple, involuntary act of drawing air into her constricted lungs, a monumental task.

"He laughed," Grandmama murmured, her voice

cracking with strain. "After he had his way, and I lay there weeping, he laughed as he tied his robe. I'd told him I was betrothed. Begged him not to…"

Her throat worked convulsively, and Grandpapa swore foully again.

"Irene, you don't have to do this," he said with tender solicitude.

"Yes, Harold, I do. The girls need to know the whole of it, most especially before Pennington arrives with his demands. I'd hoped he'd be a better man than his father and grandfather." She shook her head again. "But it seems the fruit doesn't fall far from the tree, does it?"

Precisely what Gabriella had said.

Grandmama gave her a sympathetic glance, and though Gabriella was quite certain she didn't want to know the whole of it, she must.

Her expression grave, but admirably valiant, her grandmother went on. "When I threatened to report the duke to the authorities, he laughed again, vowing no one would believe me. That if I dared to be so foolish as to attempt to blacken his name, he'd destroy Harold too. Neither of us would ever work in England again." She jutted her chin up in defiance, a gesture so like Gabriella, she couldn't help but see a degree of her own obstinance in her grandmother's posture.

And she admired the stubborn resilience and show of strength.

"So yes, Gabriella and Ophelia, we plotted and schemed so that when the opportunity arose, we could put the screws to that despicable sod." That last bit deflated her grandmother, for she too slumped into her chair. "But after all these years, the wretch has finally come back to haunt us, as he swore he would."

Another horrific thought intruded upon Gabriella's already muddled mind. "Oh, my God. If the old duke impregnated you, that means Pennington is my, my…what? Second, third cousin once removed?"

She'd never been able to keep distant relations straight, but while others might think it perfectly acceptable, the very idea of marrying a cousin appalled her. That alone ought to be sufficient to dissuade Maxwell.

"No, you're not." Grandpapa's harsh voice broke

through the anxious silence. "Irene miscarried that child. It nearly killed her, and it took over five years for her to conceive your father."

Grandmama reached for her husband's boney, age-spotted hand, and he promptly clasped her fingers. "After Henry was born," she said, "We came to realize we couldn't permit our hatred to taint our son. After all, we had Hartfordshire Court, and we determined then to put the ugliness behind us. Not to forgive, because I'm not certain either of us was capable of it, but to forge a new, happier future for ourselves."

This changed everything. Maxwell must be made aware. He must capitulate when these sordid facts were made known to him, surely. Except… "But what about the taxes, Grandpapa? The duke said you haven't paid the taxes these many years. The duchy has continued to pay them."

"As it well should. That was part of the terms of the agreement. I possessed the estate, and the duchy would continue to pay the taxes. I knew bloody well I could never afford to maintain Hartfordshire and pay the taxes too." He thumped his chair arm again. Poor tormented piece of furniture. "I have the documentation to prove what I say is true. I even made old Pennington put up the blunt for the starter herd of cattle."

Grandpapa had truly manipulated the duke. Gabriella wasn't sure whether she was appalled or grudgingly proud.

A rather wicked chuckle rattled his frail chest. "By God, how he swore at me. Called every curse known to God down upon me, and a few I'd never heard before. And yet, so desperate was he for an heir at his age, he acquiesced to my every demand."

Instinctively, Gabriella knew Maxwell would never be manipulated like that, but he also wouldn't defile women. *He'd force you to marry him and your grandfather to relinquish Hartfordshire Court.* Ironic how her grandfather and Maxwell both used the excuse they were righting a wrong. "But the ownership of Hartfordshire was never transferred or recorded at the register's office. How can that be?" she asked.

"I'll wager the nasty old duke bribed someone. A clerk or some official to *forget* to make the change,"

Ophelia put in.

Grandpapa nodded slowly. “Sounds like something that hell’s spawn would do. I’d have had no reason to check the recording after my initial visit, and I was assured everything was in order. It’s most unfortunate the current duke happened upon the journal and this sordidness came to light.”

“The tax issue would’ve eventually alerted the duke.” Honestly, it was surprising Maxwell hadn’t discovered that piece of the puzzle before this. Gabriella shook her head. “What a positively monstrous mess. A monstrous, monstrous tangle. I fear we may have to hire a solicitor.” She searched her grandfather’s lined faced. “I don’t suppose there are funds for that?”

He shifted uncomfortably, his focus sinking to his lap. “I cannot even replace the coach and team at this juncture,” he mumbled, his papery cheeks flushed with humiliation.

“I thought not,” she acknowledged with a resigned nod. “That makes me think. I forgot to tell you the duke arranged for the repair of the coach, and he also sent word to the auction houses to be on the alert for the team."

Her grandfather's regard sliced to Grandmother. "That was decent of him, but also beyond the mark." He opened his mouth as if to declare something else, but the quelling glance his wife leveled him, silenced whatever he was about to say.

How could they possibly hope to fight a wealthy duke in court?

"I cannot see that it would do any good, even if we could afford a solicitor," Ophelia ventured. "Grandpapa is correct. In circumstances like this, aristocrats always win. Justice is only for the rich and powerful."

What about the court of public opinion? The elitist circles Maxwell traveled in? What would the *haut ton* make of these juicy tidbits? Could Gabriella spin the facts and make the Dukes of Penningtons the villains and the Breckensoles the victims?

Probably, but the disgrace would ruin her family. What was more, *le beau monde*, didn't give a fig about commoners being rode roughshod over by some pompous duke. Peers were exonerated of crimes all the time with no more than a bored blink from their aristocratic compatriots.

"But if the duke *thinks* we'll make a public scandal of it, a reeking royal stink, that may well do the trick," Ophelia offered hopefully.

Gabriella could well imagine how her twin would affect that. Hadn't she suggested poisoning the duke in jest?

Maxwell had been most adamant he wanted to avoid any *on dit*. But such a scandal would reveal Grandmama's humiliation and likely settle Ophelia and Gabriella firmly on the shelf.

Besides, this was becoming a vicious cycle of extortion and retribution, and it didn't sit well with her. When would it end? She'd like to believe she and her family were above such ugliness. Maxwell too. In truth she objected more to the means by which she would be compelled to marry him than any personal objection to him.

"There is a way…" Grandmama hesitated, her mouth pressed into a tight line. "I possess something that may well do the trick."

A sick feeling cramped Gabriella's stomach, and she closed her eyes for a blink.

"What's this?" Grandpapa asked, wrinkling his forehead and probing her with his gaze. "You've kept a secret from me, Irene?"

"I have. Because the duchess was a sweet, gentle woman, forced into a marriage with a man old enough to be her grandfather. I always pitied her." She dropped her focus to her hands where she tormented the poor handkerchief. "The sixth duke," she continued softly, "beat and violated the poor woman. I cannot tell you how many times I cared for a split lip and helped her to dress to cover the bruises he inflicted upon her. The brute carried on with whores in the chamber adjoining hers. Even made her watch sometimes."

Gabriella put her palms to her churning stomach and swallowed, so sickened, she truly feared she'd cast up her accounts. Maxwell's grandfather had truly been evil, but to blackmail him in turn? It wasn't right.

"That's why she loved Hartfordshire Court so much." As Grandmama relived the events that had transpired so many years ago, her gaze went vacant again. "It was where she escaped from him and his string of strumpets. When she learned he attacked me, she'd had enough. She planned to leave him."

Grandpapa and Ophelia regarded her with expectation, and Gabriella wished herself anywhere else. As furious as she was with Maxwell, she didn't want to be a part of any scheme that inflicted harm upon him.

"You see, the duchess despised her husband, and she had a lover. I helped her arrange meetings with him." A defiant glint entered Grandmama's eyes. "I don't regret it. That poor woman deserved some small measure of happiness. I swore I'd never breathe a word, but her lover was the seventh duke's father."

13

Max turned on his heel, a cheroot gripped between his thumb and forefinger, and circled the flagstone terrace at the rear of Chartworth Hall once more. In the hours since he'd watched Gabriella—proud and magnificent as any Amazonian warrior—run away from him, taking his heart and his self-respect with her, he'd been deep in soul-searching contemplation.

Not a particularly religious man, he'd nonetheless sent several prayers skyward asking for guidance. For the ability to forgive. To know what course to take.

What had seemed just and fair a few months ago, even a few days ago, had faded into ambiguity with the knowledge he'd wounded her. Unforgivably.

You've taken up someone else's offense as your own.

I shall grow to hate you.

I could have loved you, Maxwell.

He took a long draw of the cheroot, then with a grimace tossed it to the pavers, crushing it rather viciously beneath his boot heel. He'd all but given up smoking straight out of university. He rarely indulged anymore, but this hellish day had sent him in search of a smoke, only to have him realize after two brief puffs he really couldn't abide the smell and taste. Another example of the many idiotic things men did just because someone, somewhere, at some time, thought it a splendid idea.

A bloody, disgusting idea.

Scraping a hand through his hair, not caring the least the disheveled strands would likely send his valet, Filby, into an apoplexy, Max brought his gaze up to survey the manicured lawns. Topiary hedges enclosed immaculately groomed gardens. Blossoms had begun to form on the early blooming flowers and trees, and soon their fragrance would perfume the air.

He rarely stayed at Chartworth, the memories of a lonely childhood, austere and frightened servants, a mean-spirited and perpetually soused grandfather, and a neglectful father were enough to keep him away. He'd often considered letting the estate, so he'd not be obligated to oversee it any longer.

Thank God he'd been sent to boarding school before his eighth birthday. It—and the life-long friends he'd made there, had been his saving grace. Visits home had been infrequent, dreaded, and in later years avoided. But Max had often enjoyed school breaks with other young scamps, mainly because his sire, quite frankly, didn't give a damn where he spent the holidays or summers.

He rested a hip on the elaborate balustrade while squinting into the cloudless azure sky. An unusually brilliant day for early spring in the English countryside. Beyond the hedgerow, a classic white marble garden arbor's domed roof peeked above the lavender, purple and cream lilacs and the crimson, fuchsia, and white camellias planted by his mother.

Another severely unhappy duchess.

Had any Duchess of Pennington ever been happy and content? Truly, wholly happy? Had a duke ever been? Not even he, renowned for his droll humor and teasing witticisms?

Gabriella deserved happiness.

Who was he to rob her of any chance of it?

A selfish, bastard. That was who. He'd known that all along, so why did he suddenly care?

A pair of accusing hazel eyes framed by lush lashes, momentarily blinded him.

It all came down to Gabriella Breckensole. She'd handily taken his well-thought out plans, and pitched them arse over noggin. What's more, he didn't mind nearly as much as he ought.

A slight smile quirked his mouth, and a peculiar urge to run and conceal himself in the arbor as he had as a youth gripped him. Within the stately columns, elaborate marble benches had provided the perfect backdrop for an errant boy to read his favorite books, pretend he slayed dragons and other mythical creatures, or simply hide from his latest starchy tutor or sot of a father when he'd been in his cups.

Which was most of the time.

Max's focus gravitated over the greens. He owned this. These thousands of acres. As had his father before him and his grandfather before him, and the previous generations of Pennington dukes too. Money and position and power accompanied the title, as did expectations and obligations. Max claimed all of this as his, and yet, he begrudged a simple man a few acres and the house it stood upon.

No, it is the means by which Breckensole acquired the estate I object to.

Over the decades, had his forebearers committed equally unjust crimes? One ancestor—his two times great-grandfather?—married five, increasingly younger heiresses with the sole purpose of expanding his holdings. It was rumored that not all of his duchesses had met with natural deaths.

Max roved his gaze over his lands again. Everything within his sight bespoke wealth and quality. Yet, never had Chartworth Hall felt less like a home. Never had the opulent halls and rooms rung more emptily. Never, *ever,* had he felt this lonely and hollow aching for what he'd unlikely ever have. Love. The love of a woman like Gabriella.

Who did he think he fooled? Certainly not himself. Not a woman *like* her. Her. Gabriella Fern Miriam Breckensole. He yearned for her love. Freely and willingly and wholeheartedly given.

His attention shifted to the east, toward Hartfordshire Court. He'd dine there in less than two hours. Afterward, he'd present Breckensole with the evidence that ensured the older man's ruination and thereby, guaranteed his cooperation. Only then would he explain his terms. Conditions which, he hadn't a doubt for a moment, she'd already informed her grandfather of.

The old curmudgeon would agree; after a bit of posturing and grumbling for his pride's sake.

Victory was within Max's grasp. He'd all but won. So why didn't exultation thrum through his veins? Instead, his mouth tasted acrid and bitter, and a peculiar sense of having failed in some vital way beat relentlessly against his self-respect.

Men at some time are masters of their fates.

Another damnable quote from Shakespeare. Of all the incongruous thoughts to invade his musings. For God's sake. He didn't even particularly like Shakespeare and for certain hadn't made an effort to memorize the bard's poems. He'd found the plays and sonnets tedious at best and when compelled to watch a theatrical performance of one or the other, often could barely keep his eyes open or suppress his bored yawns.

Men at some time are masters of their fates.

Was he? Could he be? Must he follow the less than praiseworthy footsteps of his ancestors? Did what had come before truly have to mold him into a callous, cold-hearted blackguard no better than the previous dukes of Pennington?

Or…could he be the one who initiated change?

If he forgave Breckensole his offense and debt, the duchy wouldn't suffer one way or the other from his decision. The dukedom, unlike many others, had plodded along quite nicely these past decades, despite the despicable dukes born into its prestigious lineage.

But the Breckensoles would suffer tremendously if

he persisted. Wasn't that what he'd wanted?

Not anymore. Gabriella's happiness mattered more than all else.

More than Father? Grandfather? Revenge?

He chuckled, lifting his face to the sky. Yes. Hell, yes! A thousand times more.

She was all that was good and decent and wonderful. Her radiant smile lit the room and shadows descended, cloying and heavy, upon his soul when she departed his presence. Could this, whatever this unfamiliar feeling heating his blood and causing his heart to beat an uneven cadence, be love? Could he, the offspring of generations of unfeeling bastards, actually be capable of love?

As Max strode indoors and climbed the risers to his rooms, his internal battle raged on.

Forgive and forget?

Punish and demand restitution?

Could he forsake the duty to his family for something as wholly selfish as love for a woman who could scarcely stand to look upon his face?

Ah, but Gabriella had kissed him. More than once.

Willingly and passionately, so she must've felt something toward him, if only desire. She wasn't a flirt nor fast, and she'd succumbed with a fervor that had startled but pleased him.

He needn't peer into a looking glass to know a satisfied grin curved his mouth.

Pausing along the second-floor gallery, he swept his gaze over the very first duke of Pennington's portrait. Complete with a neat black beard, a high-necked doublet under a dark blue and gold brocade overgown, and accented by a gaudily jeweled collar—*a truly heinous thing, actually*—his forefather stared back at him with haughty arrogance.

Prideful lot were the Dukes of Pennington. God only knew how many bastards these dukes had sired over the generations. As was typical of all the Dukes of Pennington, the first duke wore a solemn expression.

Mayhap they all had bad teeth? He ran his tongue over his own teeth, all straight except for one slightly crooked lower tooth. He faithfully cleansed them twice daily.

Hands clasped behind him, he slowly meandered

the length of the carpeted corridor, his head slanted in concentration. He studied the serious faces of his ancestors, none particularly handsome, save his sire. His father bore classical striking features: a straight blade of a nose, a high forehead, sculpted cheeks and jaw, and dark hair that women seemed to find deucedly attractive.

Max didn't include himself in that category.

His face was far too angular, his nose slightly too large with a distinct hump, and his different colored eyes had always vexed him. Not that he minded them all that much when he glanced into the cheval glass, but others seemed to find them wholly unnerving or intriguing, depending upon who the observer might happen to be.

Gabriella, he realized with a small start, had never made him self-conscious about the abnormality. Many were the times she'd looked deeply into his eyes, and not once had there been even the merest flicker in hers. But then, that was so like her. To accept people as they were, without judgment or prejudice. To see the good in them.

He suspected he could've had a gross facial disfigurement, and she'd have treated him with courtesy and kindness, nary a flinch marring her comportment.

When he at last stood before his grandfather's and father's portraits, he straightened, and with a critical eye, narrowed his gaze. They bore little resemblance to one another, except in attitude, behavior, and speech. Actually, that wasn't quite true either.

At one time, his father had wanted to pursue a military career. The navy to be precise. Max had learned of that desire during one of his father's intoxicated rants. Naturally, as the only heir, he was forbidden any such thing. He'd also been forbidden to wed the woman he loved. She'd been far beneath his station.

Max had concluded as a young lad that his father was a weak man, compelled to become something he didn't have the character or fortitude for.

He glanced back down the row of austere ancestors in their gilded frames.

By damn.

When he sat for his portrait, he was going to grin as wide as a cat in the cream, even if it meant he appeared half mad. He wouldn't pose as a somber-faced wretch looking as if death or the pox or the plague was about to descend upon him.

Except…He unclasped his hands and leaned forward. One arm bent across his waist, the elbow of the other resting upon his forearm, he cradled his chin between his finger. Except, if he continued along this course, determined to destroy Breckensole, would he have reason to smile ever again?

His vivacious Gabriella would be destroyed in the process. In that moment, the pain in his heart crested, writhing with such severity, he gasped and clutched both hands to his chest.

He couldn't do it. Couldn't exact his revenge. Not out of any misplaced mercy or grace directed toward Breckensole. Gabriella, his sweet, unpredictable, vexing Gabriella had stopped him as surely as if a royal decree had been issued.

Max loved her, and love forgave a multitude of sins. None of the other signified. It was as if he was able to finally see clearly. What mattered most was that he not destroy that incredible, remarkable, beyond comparison woman.

Pennington duty and honor could burn in the seventh layer of hell's flames, which he strongly suspected, a few of these very same ancestors might very well be doing at this moment.

He, by God above, would not further blacken the dukedom with misplaced revenge.

Gabriella had reason to hate him. He'd given her every reason to. But he would not force her into a union she didn't want. That much he could do.

At once, as if heavy, binding chains had been removed, a weight lifted from him. Melted off like a candle held to a fire. He laughed out loud, causing a passing chambermaid to give him a queer look and scuttle past him a mite faster.

He wasn't sure what he'd do about the tax situation, but Breckensole could keep Hartfordshire Court and Max would never make a claim against the estate again. He'd inform the Breckensoles of his decision at dinner. Then tomorrow, he'd be straight for

London. For staying in the vicinity, with Gabriella so close but utterly and forever unattainable was unbearable. Even for a hard-hearted Duke of Pennington.

14

At precisely seven of the clock, a leather portfolio and Gabriella's sketchpad and pencils neatly tucked beneath his left arm, Max rapped upon Hartfordshire's stout door. Dead silence met his knock, and after a couple of minutes, he pounded the door a jot harder.

He'd never been inside Hartfordshire Court and had no idea if the house's layout prevented the servants from hearing a knock upon the entrance. Another extended moment passed before the door finally swung open.

A plump, slightly breathless maid holding a candlestick bobbed a curtsy. "Your Grace." She swept her arm to the side, indicating he should enter. After setting the taper down, she managed a timid smile and accepted his hat and gloves.

"Thank you," he intoned, more formally than he'd intended. To his ears he sounded like a bloody, pompous windbag. Not the impression he wanted to make at all. He tried again, this time offering a cordial smile. "That's very kind of you."

Her unplucked eyebrows skittered upward, and she gawked at him as if he were dicked in the nob before finally murmuring, "Not at all, Your Grace."

It wasn't bloody kind of her. It was her job, as they both knew full well.

"Yes. Well…" He cleared his throat, turning his head and listening for voices. "I appreciate it nonetheless."

Now she did gape at him as if he were stark-raving mad. Dukes didn't go about complimenting servants for mundane tasks.

For God's sake, man. Shut up. You're babbling like a tabby.

"Miss Breckensole's drawing supplies." He passed

them over as well. He retained the portfolio, and though the maid eyed it curiously, didn't offer to take the case.

Were the servants aware of what tonight's visit was truly about? Entirely possible in a household of this size.

After a long blink, she placed his possessions and the sketchpad and pencils upon a marble-topped hall tree stand and collected the candlestick. "The family awaits you in the drawing room. This way, if you please."

And even if he didn't.

So Breckensole didn't even permit candles lit in the entry. More evidence of his miserliness. Still, it wasn't Max's business whether the pinch-penny lit one or a hundred candles for his guests.

Uncharacteristic nerves pattered along his spine as he followed the maid's brisk pace.

Likely, she was needed in the kitchen to finish the meal's preparation. He hadn't been surprised the Breckensoles didn't retain a butler. His man of business had reported they kept a small staff of four: A cook, this maid of all work, the injured groomsman, Jackson, and the stable lad who'd led Balor to the small stables positioned to the back and left of the main house.

The single candle threw weird, tremulous shadows along the sparsely furnished corridor. Dark wainscoting—walnut?— covered the lower third of the passageway, and faded floral wallpaper, the upper two thirds. A lone painting of a Dutch landscape interrupted the monotony.

At the drawing room door, the maid paused after sending him an uncertain glance. She knocked lightly, then leaned in and pressed the handle. "His Grace, the Duke of Pennington."

Dead silence met her announcement as four wary gazes took him in: Breckensole's blazed with hatred, his wife's blatant distrust, Miss Ophelia's accusation, and Gabriella's brimming with sadness.

I could have loved you.

"Adel," Mrs. Breckensole said. "Please light the hall sconces."

"Yes, Mrs. Breckensole." The maid dipped her

chin and after another swift glance about the tension-filled room, made her escape. No doubt the kitchen gossip would include the family's less than warm welcome.

Gabriella, wearing an extremely becoming pale pink gown trimmed in ivory lace, her hair piled atop her head with jaunty curls framing her face, and pearl earbobs dangling from her dainty ears had never appeared more lovely. Slightly pale, but supremely composed, Gabriella being Gabriella, broke the awkward silence.

She sunk into a graceful curtsy which Max acknowledged with a bow. "Your Grace, I believe you are already acquainted with my grandfather, Harold Breckensole."

Not exactly acquainted. There'd never been a formal introduction in all the years their properties had paralleled each other. They'd seen the other in the distance, of course, but the first unfortunate meeting had occurred the other night. Nevertheless, determined to be at his most charming for her sake, he angled his head. "Sir."

He received a stony glower in greeting.

Splendid. Things were off to a romping, jolly good start.

Gabriella's mouth flattened minutely, and he could've sworn she sent her grandfather a reproachful glance. *Easier to catch flies with honey and all that*, her silent message implied.

She was all the sweetness Max needed to persuade him to do almost anything.

"Please permit me to introduce my grandmother. Your Grace, Irene Breckensole. Grandmama, Maxwell, Duke of Pennington." Simple and direct without embellishment or pretense.

He bent into a formal bow, and Mrs. Breckensole deemed to lower her chin a fraction. Something in the handsome woman's frosty gaze sent prickles of unease up and down his spine.

Neither Mr. or Mrs. Breckensole had bothered to rise as he was accustomed to, and he wasn't certain whether he was more amused that his title didn't impress them in the least or miffed at their insolence. Then again, Mrs. Breckensole was still recovering from her bout of ill health.

Her husband, on the other hand, was just being an ornery ass. In a word, himself.

Max angled toward Miss Ophelia and bowed again. "Miss Ophelia."

"Duke." Her curtsy was so shallow as to be just this side of rude.

What had he expected? That they'd be giddy he'd deemed to call upon them?

Another stilted silence filled the room—evidently the fire the only thing capable of moving or showing any degree of cheer. Hell, Breckensole had yet to speak a word, although had his glare been a weapon, Max would've been eviscerated upon entrance.

Gabriella tapped her toes, back and forth, back and forth. Was she even aware she had that nervous quirk? When she caught sight of his slight grin and his pointed stare at her slippers, she stopped at once. Rather than off-putting or annoying, he found the trait endearing.

Wasn't he a completely besotted bumble-brain? And it was quite the most puzzling, incredible thing.

Still, his reason for being here wasn't pleasant. He breathed out a silent sigh. There was no point in waiting until after dinner and extending everyone's discomfort to say what he'd come to say. Lacing his fingers together behind his back, he splayed his legs. "I think it best for all if I speak directly."

Breckensole snorted, and Miss Ophelia placed a hand on her grandmother's shoulder in a reassuring fashion.

"Wouldn't you prefer to wait until after we've dined?" The look Gabriella leveled him suggested she thought whatever he had to say might put them off their food.

Or maybe they plan on poisoning me and thereby eliminating their problem altogether. Max wasn't serious, of course. She would never countenance such malevolent behavior.

Breckensole, on the other hand, certainly appeared up to the task. Max eyed the man's fingers, looking for a poison ring. The safe at Chartworth Hall contained one, and he'd always wondered which duke it had belonged to and if he'd ever used if for nefarious means.

Harnessing his wayward thoughts, he procured his diplomat's smile, and Gabriella's eyes rounded then shrank into contemplative slits. "I've had all afternoon to *reconsider"*—he made certain to emphasize the word— "the circumstances, and I've concluded—"

Harold Breckensole made a hostile, animalistic sound deep in his throat. With some effort, he stood and stabbed a wobbly finger at him. "We know precisely what *your* ignoble intentions are, you blackguard. But before you proceed with your demands, you had best read this." He produced a wrinkled, yellowed rectangle from within his outdated coat pocket; the fabric a peculiar faded brown much like weak tea.

A letter?

Holding the scrap of paper as if it were a rapier, a smug smile wreathed Breckensole's face.

"Grandpapa, I thought we agreed to wait until after we'd dined." Gabriella clasped her hands, tension making her fine cheekbones stand out. The smattering of light freckles on her nose contrasted starkly against her alabaster face.

"Why? Let's be done with this falderol and the false niceties. We can all appreciate this is not a social call, no matter how politely masked." Breckensole waved the foolscap, and it crackled in protest. "Then I can send this bounder on his way, eat my dinner, and actually enjoy my meal."

When Max made no effort to cross the room to accept whatever the correspondence was, she glided forward, the epitome of womanly grace. She'd have made a magnificent duchess, and his heart panged again that it would never be so. He'd had but one chance for this woman's love, and in his mistaken quest for honor, he'd callously dashed it to ribbons.

She accepted the paper from her grandfather. Edging that obstinate little chin up, she crossed to where Max stood, her skirts swishing around her ankles. Ankles which he knew to be dainty and well-formed. Lips slightly pursed, which only served to remind him he'd tasted their deliciousness but a few hours ago, she held the letter before her.

"I do believe it would be beneficial for you to read

this before you proceed." Over her shoulder, she spared her grandmother a short, pointed glance before addressing him again. "I only learned of this particular after I returned home today, else I would've apprised you of its existence."

Gratitude for her loyalty, no matter how misplaced, bloomed behind his ribs. She tried indirectly to warn him, and that could only mean the contents were rather damning. From Breckensole's gloating smirk, rather somewhat more than damning, Max would vow.

Something close to compassion tinged her self-assurance, but she met his gaze straight on. Fearless, was his Gabriella. He'd never known a time it wasn't so.

"What is it?" He skeptically eyed the note clasped between her fingers. No name or address appeared on its aged face, and mustiness wafted upward from the crumpled missive.

"It's a letter, Your Grace," Mrs. Breckensole put in, her tone clipped and guarded. "Written by your grandmother when she was the duchess."

He jerked his head up from inspecting the paper. First, he searched her gratified countenance before gravitating his focus to Breckensole's smug expression that all but screeched, "*I've-got-you-by-the-ballocks-now.*" Prickles of unease zipped along Max's spine for the third time in less than a half hour, and goose pimples raised from wrist to shoulder. He laid his portfolio on a nearby chair then studiously brushed a piece of lint from his sleeve.

He wasn't going to like this.

After a side-eyed glance at Gabriella and her twin, he flexed his jaw.

No, he wasn't going to like this in the least. He still intended to relinquish all claim to Hartfordshire Court, so whatever the letter said was moot.

He hoped.

"Your Grace." Gabriella fluttered the missive toward him, and he reluctantly accepted it.

"Why would you be in possession of a letter from my grandmother, Mrs. Breckensole?" he asked.

"I was her companion before I married." Mrs. Breckensole patted Ophelia's hand still resting upon the elderly woman's shoulder. "She trusted me absolutely, because she knew I'd never betray her. I was to have delivered that letter, but a series of calamitous events prevented my doing so."

That sent his eyebrows crashing together. How had his man of business not uncovered that detail? That very vital detail, indeed? Even now, Mrs. Breckensole defended his grandmother, and that more than anything, convinced him she spoke the truth.

Spine rigid, jaw tight, and white-knuckled hands clasped before her, Miss Ophelia claimed a spot on the striped sofa. That she felt the need to sit disturbed him even more.

He turned the missive over, searching for a name or address or anything on the reverse side. *Nothing.* That suggested something clandestine. Warning bells began to toll, first a gentle chime, but gradually increasing into a discordant cacophony. "To whom did she entrust you to deliver the letter?"

Breckensole planted his palms on his thighs, leaned forward, and blurted, "Reverend Michael Shaw. Her lover, and your father's *true* sire."

Those last four words, ringing extraordinarily loudly in the similarly unnaturally still room, tilted Max's world on its axis. His hearing grew muffled, as if he'd submerged beneath the bathwater. He shook his head to dislodge the wool and hauled his focus to Gabriella, silently asking for confirmation that he'd heard correctly.

Even before pity softened her eyes and framed her mouth, he appreciated he had. Heard every damning word perfectly clearly.

Reverend Michael Shaw was killed in a duel. Margaret is dead. She was with child.

His grandfather's journal entries also confirmed the truth.

Compassion shone on Gabriella's face.

After all Max put her through and had threatened to do, she commiserated with him? It only reinforced her goodness, and the oddest urge to laugh engulfed him. Instead, he unfolded the worn, thickly creased paper, the rustling oddly ominous. Only the longcase clock in the corner's *tick-tocking* disturbed the dense quiet.

That and Breckensole's heavy breathing. The air whistled in and out of his nose in a fashion that made Max yearn to offer his handkerchief and demand the old man blow heartily. Or take a pair of embroidery scissors to his hair-clogged nostrils and groom a pathway the air might enter and exit through with a greater degree of ease.

Training his attention on the short missive, he recognized the penmanship as that which he'd seen inside the cover of numerous books within Chartworth's extensive library. His grandmother's delicate, rather flourishing hand.

The note was short. A mere two lines: A time and location for a clandestine meeting. Grandmother and this Michael Shaw had planned to run away together.

Max read it again. And again. And again.

Off guard, his lungs cramping as if he'd been kicked in the ribs by a team of draft horses, he meticulously refolded the note. Doing so gave him something to focus on besides the tumult careening about in his head and his inability to draw anything but little puffs of air into his lungs.

Grandmother had meant to leave his grandfather. Father wasn't Grandfather's progeny.

His head spun from trying to sift fact from fallacy, and again, an absurd urge to laugh assailed him. "But why is the letter still in your possession?" he at last managed to ask. No hint of the turmoil within reached his modulated voice.

"I never had a chance to deliver it. As I said, circumstances prevented my doing so." Sadness tempered Mrs. Breckensole's tone.

"Why not?" What other shocks awaited him?

She stared into space; sorrow etched upon her aged features. She'd cared for his grandmother. Truly cared for her. The knowledge startled and humbled him.

"Somehow your grandfather learned that they intended to run away, and he challenged the reverend to a duel." She shifted her gaze to him for a moment. "I doubt the man had ever touched a pistol, let alone fired one, and the duke likely knew it as well."

Max swallowed the bile burning his throat.

"It was to have been to first blood." Mrs.

Breckensole shifted her focus away again. "But the reverend died instantly from a bullet to his heart. Sorrow drove the duchess slightly mad, and she attacked her husband. Tried to stab him with a letter opener."

"Holy God," Max whispered.

She jutted her chin upward, reminding him of Gabriella. "I witnessed the act myself and sorely wished she'd succeeded. The duke locked her in her chamber for a month, permitting no visitors, no bathwater, no fires or candles, and only gruel and stale bread for her to eat." Her voice grew raspy and her eyes watery. "Such cruelty to that gentle soul, and she was with child too."

God, his grandfather had been a tyrant. A fiend. Surely his soul had been blacker than the devil's himself.

It didn't escape Max that his grandfather's journal had made no mention of any of this. What else had he left out? Neither did it pass his notice that Mrs. Breckensole had been crafty enough to know that such a letter might be of worth at a later date. What other reason could there be for hiding it away for decades? He was about to ask that very question, when her next words tied his tongue.

"I've always suspected he pushed her down the stairs and to her death in one of his fits of rage. For that babe she carried wasn't his either." She looked straight at Max, her eyes slits of accusation and condemnation. "'Twas guilt and a raging fury that he was forced to claim another's seed as his heir that turned him into a drunkard and opium addict. Not devastation."

15

The emotions skating across Maxwell's face tore at Gabriella's composure. She'd wanted him to be taken down a notch, longed for him to understand how she felt, but this comeuppance brought her no joy. No sense of satisfaction. Because the plain, inarguable truth was, when he hurt, so did she.

A fierce, ache burned in the depths of her being. And that suggested she was beyond—way beyond, in fact—*I could have loved you Maxwell* and had come full circle to, *I do love you. So very much, that each beat of my heart is agony.*

Statue stiff, he clenched the paper. His eyelids drifted closed, the fringe of his lashes, thick and dark across his high cheekbones. He didn't argue, which suggested he believed the letter's legitimacy. The long ago, undelivered note to a lover now fisted in his grip might well be what it took for him to cry off. To change his mind about reclaiming Hartfordshire Court, marriage to her, and all the rest.

This was the miracle she'd prayed for. The means to save her home and her family. So why did tears blur her vision? Why did she want to wrap her arms around Maxwell and comfort him?

"Gabriella, take the letter before he destroys it," her grandfather ordered, a hint of panic in his tone as if the thought had just occurred to him.

"Grandfather, you're being churlish. The duke is too much of a gentleman to do any such thing." She astounded herself by defending Maxwell. She meant what she'd said though, knowing it to be the truth.

"Here, Gabriella." Arm stiff, he extended the crumpled parchment.

Her grandfather released a derisive snort following Maxwell's declaration. "Ah, yes, because you're descended from such noble blood you wouldn't destroy evidence? Yet you intended to force us from our home and blackmail my granddaughter into wedding you. And you presume to use her given name without leave?"

A slight flush tinged Maxwell's cheeks. "I beg your pardon for overstepping, Miss Breckensole. I spoke without thinking."

She bit the inside of her cheek against the urge to tell him she didn't mind.

How she despised this—seeing him defeated—every bit as much as she'd hated the uncompromising position he'd placed her in this morning. Grandfather's reveling rankled, and once she'd accepted the fragile rectangle and placed it upon the table beside her grandmother, she peered out the window. Or else she might say something wholly disrespectful to the man who'd raised her and her sister.

Nightfall obscured the garden view, but the unending darkness was preferable to seeing the pain and dismay etched on Maxwell's face. To observing this normally unflappable, composed man with his dry wit and spirited ripostes reduced to whatever wretched state this was.

Besides, what he'd intended was a far cry from disregarding the rules of dueling and slaying his opponent or shoving an *enceinte* woman down a flight of stairs. Even after everything he'd said and done, when he'd been an unmitigated cad, she yearned to smooth the angst from his features.

He'd received a monumental blow.

Not as appalling as what Grandmama had endured. Gabriella hugged her arms around her shoulders against a sudden chill.

Legally, it was of no account whether Michael Shaw or the sixth duke had sired Maxwell's father. He'd been born in wedlock, and the duke had acknowledged him as his son. Under the eyes of the law, he'd been the legal heir.

She angled toward Maxwell. She would've spared him this had she been able to.

Beneath his neatly tied cravat, his Adam's apple moved up and down, as if he struggled to control is emotions. Was he terribly disappointed? Shocked? Furious?

His attention lit upon her and rested there, his expression revealing nothing of the turbulent emotions he must surely feel. His imperious gaze, the blue eye darkened to indigo and the other a deep forest green, regarded her keenly. As if he searched for something within her eyes. Within her.

What did he seek?

The love she'd hidden from him all these months? His trust? Forgiveness? They were his for the asking.

"If you try to either force my granddaughter into marriage or to take Hartfordshire Court from us, *Your Grace,*" Grandpapa spat with such contempt, Gabriella spun to stare at him, aghast, "I shall make that letter public. Along with other unsavory information we haven't yet discussed."

"Harold, no!" Grandmama gasped, clutching her neck and spearing him a stricken look. "You cannot."

"Grandpapa, your speech and attitude do our family a disservice." Gabriella could scarce believe her boldness, but he'd gone beyond the mark. "The duke has been the epitome of politesse, and we would all do well to model him. Disagreements can be solved without lowering ourselves to petty bickering."

Another round of tomb-like silence followed her scold.

Ophelia studiously examined the worn carpet, brushing at a stain with her slipper toe. Grandmama looked askance at her husband, and to Gabriella's astonishment, Grandpapa flushed, ran a finger around the edge of his neckcloth, and with the very merest downward flicker of his eyes, acquiesced.

The inner corners of Maxwell's eyebrows lashed together as he swung his attention between her and her grandparents.

Gabriella offered a small, encouraging smile.

"There's no need for further shocks or unpleasant disclosures, I assure you. I came tonight with the intention of informing you that I've changed my mind. I've concluded that no good can come of pursuing the course I had intended to embark upon." Formality weighted his speech, but a tinge of pain colored the jagged edges of his stilted words. Although he addressed everyone, his regard remained on her. "There are additional particulars that preclude me taking the action I'd originally contemplated."

Such as?

He couldn't possibly know about Grandmama's ordeal. He'd been so unrelenting only a few hours ago. What then, in the whole of England, had been compelling enough to change his mind since this morning?

She examined the planes of his beloved face and searched his eyes for any hint. She ought to be overjoyed. This was exactly the reprieve she'd hoped for. So why, fiend seize it, did tears burn behind her eyelids and her throat twinge? Her emotions had become as fickle as a spring breeze. "You've truly changed your mind?"

Maxwell's gaze caressed her, and he gave a scant nod.

"Yes. I've come to see the error of my ways, so to speak. I shall lay no claim to Hartfordshire Court." He motioned to the forgotten leather portfolio. "All of the necessary documentation is within. My man of business will ensure the deed is properly recorded as it should have been done decades ago. Only the issues of the taxes remain to be addressed."

"I have the original documents signed by your grandfather that ensure the duchy maintains the tax liability for as long as my wife and I live." Pleasantly civil, so much so that Gabriella nearly gaped, Grandpapa gestured toward the door. "They are in my study."

That took Maxwell aback, and he blinked. "Why would he…?" Lowering his head, he cupped his nape. At last he glanced up, the earlier tumult in his eyes replaced by calculated blandness. "I presume there are other unsavory factors that warranted such benevolence?"

"Indeed, there were, Your Grace," Grandmama stated with regal dignity, a glimmer of the striking woman she'd once been surfacing.

She and Maxwell exchanged an intense, speaking glance, and something flashed in his eyes. Again, he gave the slightest acknowledgement with a half-blink and the merest downward slant of his chin.

"I believe I begin to understand. I also truly, and sincerely, regret that I may have greatly wronged you."

His gaze swept the room, lingering the longest on Gabriella. "I should've approached this matter as a gentleman rather than hurl accusations and contemplate retribution. I am not proud of my behavior and most humbly ask, that in time, perhaps you'll be able to forgive me."

She only just managed to keep her mouth from unhinging. She did, however, blink several times overcome by joy and relief.

Maxwell had apologized. Honestly. And he'd asked for forgiveness. Did dukes ever do such things? This one had, and another powerful wave of love for him throttled from her belly to her throat.

"Forgiveness?" Grandpapa suddenly laughed, slapping his knee in genuine glee. He laughed so fervently, he swiped at his eyes. "Oh, this is too perfect."

She exchanged a worried look with Ophelia. Had the strain been too much that he'd snapped and lost his faculties?

Shoulders shaking, he wrestled his mirth under control and managed between chuckles, "I've just realized his high-and-mightiness there is the grandson of a reverend. And you, Gabriella, are the granddaughter of a vicar. What a wicked sense of humor Providence has."

What a peculiar thing to say. She said as much. "Grandpapa, I hardly think such talk is appropriate or relevant."

"If I might have a look at the documentation you mentioned, Mr. Breckensole?" Posture rigid and jaw taut, Maxwell sliced an impatient glance to the door whilst flexing his fingers. Clearly, he couldn't wait to be on his way. "You may peruse mine as well."

For the first time since Maxwell had arrived, her grandfather deemed to behave like the gentleman she knew him capable of being. Likely because he had the upper hand and well knew it. "Certainly, Your Grace. Irene, please ask Cook to hold dinner until I'm finished."

"I shall do so at once." Grandmama rose, as did Ophelia. "Your Grace, you're certain you won't stay and dine with us?" She, too, must have decided a truce of some sort had been called between the Breckensoles and him.

He gave Gabriella an intense stare but declined with slight shifting of his gaze. "No, but I thank you."

"Perhaps another time?" My, wasn't her grandmother all solicitousness now? Keeping the dark secrets she and Grandpapa had harbored these many years no doubt had been a tremendous burden and to be free of them at last, quite liberating.

He shook his head. "I fear not. I'm for London first thing tomorrow and don't anticipate returning to Chartworth."

Ever? Or just not in the near future? Or distant future?

Once more his gaze found Gabriella's, and such regret shone in his eyes, she nearly gasped. *Don't go. We need to talk,* she wanted to cry. Naturally, she couldn't. What could she say with her grandparents and sister staring on, in any event?

I don't want you to leave? I want to explore what this thing is between us? Yes, you've been a knave, and I most probably ought to detest you, but my stupid, stupid, stupid heart insists on loving you instead.

I beg you. Do not leave me behind. Give me a chance to ask for your forgiveness, for I've wronged you as well.

No, she couldn't confess something so private in front of her family. But she most assuredly would find a way to speak with Maxwell before he left. And that would be no easy task. She jutted her chin out, only the tiniest bit, lest anyone notice the determined spark she was certain glinted in her eyes.

"Girls, come along." Grandmama extended her elbows, indicating each twin should take one. "Your grandfather and the duke have important matters to discuss."

How Gabriella wanted to object. She wracked her brain for a feasible excuse to stay. She might argue the women should be permitted to be a part of the discussion since Hartfordshire would pass to her and her sister one day. Wouldn't it? She had always presumed as much, but nothing of the kind had ever been suggested.

For certain she didn't want to toddle down that bumpy road with the duke listening.

What then?

Perchance…? She slid Ophelia a contemplative side-eyed look. Yes. It might work. If she was careful. She tapped her toe once, then promptly stopped. She'd give herself away if she weren't careful.

Maxwell bowed. "Ladies."

Even Grandmama deemed to sink into a curtsy.

"Your Grace," the women murmured in unison.

Another refrain pealed in Gabriella's head. *Don't go. Don't go. Please. Don't go.* Her feet carried her forward, despite her protesting mind, and she gained the corridor.

Adel had lit the sconces as directed. Well, two of them. It was unheard of for the Breckensole household to waste six candles in one evening to light the passageway, even for a duke. Halfway down the corridor, she slowed her steps, closed her eyes, and pressed her fingertips between her eyebrows.

"Grandmama?" She concentrated on sounding breathless and feeble.

"Yes, dear?" Her grandmother quizzically peered up. "Why, Gabriella, are you quite all right?"

She shook her head. "I don't believe I am. I'm not feeling at all well and urgently need to lie down."

Worry folding her features like a fan, Grandmama *tisked* and *tutted.*

"This has been too much of a strain for you. Thinking one moment to protect your family and enter into a horrid union, and then learning all of these sordid particulars no woman with delicate sensibilities ought ever to hear. I cannot say as I blame you." She patted Gabriella's cheek. "Go along. Change into your nightclothes, and I'll have a simple tray sent up later if you are feeling more yourself."

Gabriella caught Ophelia's eye. "Come with me," she mouthed above their grandmother's head.

An imperceptible flicker of Ophelia's lashes suggested she understood. "Grandmama, permit me to help Gabriella. I'll come down straightaway once she's settled."

A smile arced their grandmother's lined face. "I sometimes forget how close the two of you are. Go along, Ophelia. I suspect your grandfather will be several minutes more in any event. I don't know how I shall pacify Cook. She was quite put upon, having to prepare a meal worthy of a duke on such short notice, and when she learns he's not staying to dine, I truly fear she may give notice."

Gabriella bent and kissed her grandmother's cheek. "I'm sure you can console her adequately."

"Let us hope so, for as we all know, I am a dismal cook." She chuckled, in the best humor Gabriella had seen her in for some time.

She didn't exaggerate. Ophelia and Gabriella could do a kitchen justice if required to do so, but Grandmama's talents were with a needle or a hairbrush and hair pins, not a pot and spoon.

Once in her chamber, Gabriella made straight for her wardrobe. Before Ophelia had finished closing the door, she'd pulled out a simple gown and her half boots.

"What are you about?" Ophelia demanded, crossing her arms. "Hasn't there been enough chaos and calamity for one day?"

"I must speak with Maxwell before he leaves. I'll await him in the stables." Gabriella presented her back.

"Now, do hurry and unfasten me. I'm counting on you to keep my confidence and to prevent Grandmama from checking upon me too." Impatient and fearing he'd leave before she caught him, she glanced over her shoulder.

Ophelia hadn't moved but regarded her with a rather too astute stare. A fine eyebrow crept upward and a hint of amusement played about her mouth. "Maxwell?"

Oh, piddle. His name had slipped out without Gabriella even noticing.

"Oh, Gabby. You *do* care for him." Suddenly, she grinned and rushed to Gabriella. "I knew it. Naturally, when he was being so very beastly and impossibly ducal, you couldn't agree to marry him. I confess, I do quite like him despite his being a Pennington," she declared as she swiftly unfastened the hooks holding Gabriella's gown shut. "And I think he's good for you."

Good for me?

Yes, he was.

In short order, Gabriella had changed and donned

her simple woolen cloak. Holding hands, the sisters stepped into the empty passage. On tiptoes, Gabriella hurried to the landing, carefully leaning over to inspect the blessedly empty foyer below.

Ophelia winked, giving a cheeky grin. “I’ll go first and signal when all is clear.” She was enjoying this misadventure too much. “This is jolly good fun,” she whispered, grabbing Gabriella’s hand and giving her cold fingers a squeeze.

Gabriella hadn’t thought to don her gloves. She’d been in too much of a hurry. There wasn’t time to go back for them now, however. Maxwell might depart at any moment.

“Just don’t do something foolish and impulsive such as elope with him.” A tiny frown scrunched Ophelia’s nose. “Grandmama and Grandpapa would never let me out of the house again. I’d die here, a prune of an old maid.” She squeezed Gabriella’s hand again. “Besides, I want to see you marry. Promise me, Gabby.”

If Maxwell asked her to trot off to Scotland, Gabriella would. Indeed, she would.

"I don't think there's any chance of that, Fee," she murmured, wishing with all of her heart that there was.

Scandal be damned.

16

Five minutes later, Gabriella carefully slipped into the stables. Maxwell's horse poked his majestic head over the stall door, raising it up and down, almost in an equine bow. A long swoosh of breath blew past her lips.

Thanks be to God, he hadn't left yet,

A lone lantern hung on a peg, lighting the tidy barn. Grandpapa would have a tantrum if he knew. Wanton waste and all that. But Davy had likely thought, and rightly so, a duke worthy of a bit of light.

Of the stable hand, there was no sign. That was also a welcome blessing.

He'd probably fallen asleep in his quarters already. Up before dawn every day, he worked hard—

too hard—and usually sought his bed after sundown. As the Breckensoles never had guests in the evening, Davy had probably assumed it quite gracious to provide a light before he found his mattress.

Tomorrow, Gabriella would speak to him about the danger of leaving a lantern unattended and about expectations for attending guests' horseflesh. The duke shouldn't have to see to saddling his mount. However, she wouldn't scold too severely since the young man's absence provided her with the perfect opportunity to speak with Maxwell alone.

She hadn't any idea what she would say. There'd been no time to rehearse. And yet here she stood, unwilling for them to part with so much unsaid between them.

The horse lifted his head again, his great brown eyes watching her.

She greeted the other two horses before making her way to his stall. "Hello, handsome boy. I never did thank you for the ride the other night. It was most gentlemanly of you to accommodate two riders."

At the mention of that sensual ride, any remaining

denial ebbed, and her true feelings flooded upon her like a massive ocean wave. Overwhelming, powerful, and wholly inescapable.

Maxwell had been absolutely right.

Attraction *had* sparked between them from the onset. The magnetism had steadily grown into something more over these past months, strengthened upon every encounter, and had culminated this last week. Had all of her attempts to ignore and slight him at every turn been more of an internal battle to fight her escalating fascination? Because, though her head said she should detest him for what she'd discovered, her heart had a mind of its own and frankly refused to cooperate.

Running a hand over Balor's neck, she murmured, "How can I tell Maxwell any of that? Hmm?"

"Tell me what?"

A hand to her throat, she whirled to face the entrance. "You startled me, Maxwell." It came out a strangled squeak, and she cursed inwardly for stating the obvious and for sounding like an oversized mouse.

Marked uncertainty shadowing his features, he

lingered a foot inside the door. He'd donned neither his hat nor gloves, but held them in his left hand.

She permitted herself a leisurely perusal of this ebony-haired powerful lion of a man, from impressively wide shoulders, to a narrow waist, long well-muscled thighs, and calves ensconced in midnight Hessians. Her gaze made the return journey, every bit as enjoyable as the first, until her attention rested upon the molded planes of his dear face.

Perhaps, she also permitted her focus to hover on his lips as she recalled the kisses they'd shared. If she closed her eyes, she imagined she could feel his lips upon hers still.

Gabriella's heart gave a queer flutter. She loved him.

Had loved him since…Well, she didn't know exactly when he'd entered her heart and set up house without so much as a by-your-leave. But he had entrenched himself there. Had taken over, and now Maxwell, the eighth Duke of Pennington, had absolute rule of the organ.

What's more, she didn't mind at all, and she

wouldn't object in the least if he felt the same. But did a lady just come out with it? Ask a gentleman if he loved her too? If that was the reason he'd changed his mind about seizing Hartfordshire Court before learning of his grandmother's letter?

But what if he didn't love her? What if his only interests were Hartfordshire and lust for her body? Straightening her shoulders, she brought her chin up. She'd know the truth, at least. That was something. Everything.

A hint of vulnerability creased the corners of his eyes. "You shouldn't be out here, Gabriella."

Not chérie or minx or vixen?

She almost bit her lip and had actually lifted her right toe before she caught herself.

He shook his head and took a pace forward. "It's not—"

"Done?" she shrugged, and forming her mouth into a disinterested *moue,* brushed her hand down Balor's neck. "I know. But, you see, Maxwell, I wanted to speak with you before you left. I feared that after you departed for London on the morrow, it might be some time before you returned. *If*, you returned at all." Nothing too terribly subtle about that. Would he understand the meaning in her words she wanted him to?

"And that distresses you?" After setting his possessions on a low stool, he prowled nearer.

Swallowing, she managed a small nod. "Yes, I find that it does. Very much, in fact."

He was upon her now, and she pulled her gaze upward from his waistcoat, past his starched neckcloth and the ruby pin twinkling there, over the light stubble shadowing his strong chin, to his firm mouth then higher still until she met his gaze.

The intensity of those hot eyes sent a sensual shiver jolting to her knees, which had inconveniently decided to take this moment to become the consistency of strawberry flummery.

"Why, may I ask?" His regard sank to her mouth.

Was he also remembering their passionate embraces?

"I find the idea of you leaving for a lengthy stretch quite distresses me." Good Lord, could she sound anymore prim or tight-laced?

He brushed her cheek with his finger, then her jaw, then the seam of her lips. "Why?"

She tingled all over, and he appeared as cool as the proverbial cucumber. *Blast the man.* He wasn't making this easy.

Shouldn't a gentleman, a duke for goodness sake, do the gallant thing and declare himself first? But what if he believed the gentlemanly thing was to let her make the choice, because before, he hadn't given her an option?

Gabriella grasped his lapels, running her fingertips along the fine fabric. "I shall miss you beyond measure. Quite unbearably, truth to tell. And I don't wish to be miserable every day, wondering when you will return. *If* you will return." He started to open his mouth, but she quickly put a finger to his lips. "Don't you dare ask me why again," she ordered, low and husky.

At that, he cocked an eyebrow, maddeningly wicked and self-assured, and had the gall to nip her finger before capturing it in his palm and whispering,

"Why?" his voice deep and gravelly and seductive.

Standing on her toes, she cupped his nape. "Because, you obnoxious, irritating man, I love you."

The very instant that I saw you, did my heart fly to your service.

What an appropriate time to remember a line from Shakespeare.

With a rough groan, Maxwell swept her into his arms, capturing her mouth in a scorching kiss that promptly sent every coherent thought in her brain straight out of her mind. He gripped her bottom, pushing his rigid length into her belly, and devoured her mouth.

Time stood perfectly still as they explored the other's mouth between whispers of adoration and heartfelt apologies. A hunger and yearning swirled within her, increasing in intensity, until she made little mewling sounds against his lips.

"Maxwell, please," she pleaded, for what she didn't know.

A horse snorted in what very much sounded like an equestrian chuckle, and Maxwell finally lifted his head.

She cried out in protest, trying to claim his lips once more.

His features strained and eyes hooded, he shook his head. He rested his forehead against hers. "No, *mon amour*. I'm almost beyond restraint, and I refuse to tup the future Duchess of Pennington in a pile of straw."

She didn't think the idea so very awful. In fact… "Perhaps not the first time, but mayhap *some* time?" she asked coyly.

He growled low in his throat and nipped her neck. "Vixen. Siren. Temptress. Minx." Smoothing errant strands of hair from her cheek, his gaze so tender, she wanted to weep, he asked hesitantly, "Do you truly love me?" Awe, wonder, and disbelief blended together to make the question harsh and raspy.

"I do, Maxwell." She put a palm to his cheek. "I truly do. I've loved you for so long, but I was so hurt and angry, I refused to see it. Stubbornly refused to acknowledge what I knew to be true."

Something wondrous lit in his eyes, and he pressed a reverent kiss to her forehead then encircled her with his arms.

"And you'll marry me? Because you want to?" He spoke against her hair, his lips a warm caress. "I cannot imagine ever loving another woman as I do you. And if you should refuse me, I'll understand. I shall, truly, because I doubt your grandparents will ever agree to the match. They might even cut you off and forbid you to see me." His embraced tightened. "But I shall never wed, then. I'll carry you in my heart until I draw my last breath, Gabriella, my love."

"I'll gladly marry you." She smiled up into his face, caressing his bristly jaw. "Without regret, whether or not my grandparents' consent. Although, I suspect they'll be amendable as long as they know I wed you of my own free will. I love you, dear man."

Emotion choked his ragged voice, and he swallowed audibly, pressing his cheek into her hair. "No one… No one has ever said they loved me before."

A broken cry escaped her, and tears leaked from her eyes. "Oh, my darling. I shall tell you every day upon awakening, every night upon going to sleep in your arms, and a thousand times in between. I love you. I love you. I love you."

He tilted her chin upward until their eyes met. "Forgive me, Gabriella. I was an utter fool. The things your grandfather revealed to me tonight…" He closed his eyes. "Well, let's just say I'm profoundly glad the sixth Duke of Pennington's blood *does not* flow through my veins."

"I regret you had to learn that ugliness," she whispered.

"I'm not," he said quite fiercely. "It's a relief. I've often thought my father and I were somehow different than the previous dukes. Now I know why."

"It's all so sad, really."

"How long must I wait to make you my wife?" Maxwell smiled into her eyes, and she wanted to weep from joy. To shout her jubilation. To take him to her bed right then and there.

Head angled, she tipped her mouth upward. "I believe you mentioned a special license?"

"I did, indeed, *chérie*."

"Then I choose tomorrow, by the river where you

first kissed me." She clasped his hand, bringing to her heart. "Shall we tell the others our good news?"

"I'll need a fortifying kiss before I interrupt your grandfather's dinner," Maxwell claimed, mischief and desire playing across his mouth. "The man fairly terrifies me."

Gabriella was happy to oblige for several long and most delicious minutes.

London, England

Late April, 1810

Lilting music filled his ears as Max guided his wife of just over a month around the sanded parquet floor of Mathias, Duke of Westfall's ballroom. Invitations had awaited them upon their arrival in London, and a steady stream continued to pour into the Mayfair manor every day. News of his nuptials had traveled throughout London's elite circles with prodigious speed.

Upon his first foray to *Bon Chance*, after being heartily congratulated, the dukes of Asherford,

Westfall, Bainbridge, and San Sebastian had taken him aside for a finger's worth of brandy. Unwed themselves, each had teased him unmercifully about having been snared by the parson's mousetrap.

"Yes, and now that I'm off the Marriage Mart, my friends, there's one less peer for those title-hungry huntresses' to snare. You'd best be on your guard, lest you find yourselves saying, 'I do.'"

They'd cursed him for the worst sort of friend for even suggesting such a wretched thing. But like Max, each knew full well he was expected to marry and produce an heir, no matter how reluctant they were to enter the blissful state of matrimony.

A primal smile bent Max's mouth. Those gents could mock all they wanted, but he had no complaints whatsoever. His wonderful, unpredictable Gabriella was every bit as capricious inside as outside the bedchamber. That promised tumble in the hay had proven quite invigorating. As had the delightful joining in the library yesterday and the exhilarating tussle in the carriage the day before. Each and every one initiated by his seductress of a wife.

Yes, indeed, God had smiled upon him the day he'd met this enticing armful he now called wife. "Enjoying yourself, Duchess?" He adored calling her that and seeing the pink bloom in her cheeks.

"You well know I am." She discreetly craned her elegant neck. "So are Ophelia and Jessica Brentwood." She slid her eyes sideways, and he followed her glance.

Ophelia danced with a dashing ship's captain, and the Duke of Kincade, only arrived from the Highlands last week, skillfully swept Jessica amongst the other dancers.

"And Rayne Wellbrook and Sophronie Slater too." Gabriella tipped her head toward the young women. "Though, honestly, they look slightly more terrified than excited."

"The Season can be a bit daunting for those unaccustomed to it." He would've eschewed most of the invitations they'd received, but as Gabriella had never had a Come Out or a Season, he felt compelled to allow her to attend whatever routs, soirees, balls, and other assemblies she desired.

The set ended, and she excused herself to use the lady's retiring room. Halfway across the floor, Nicolette Twistleton, Miss Ophelia, and Everleigh, Duchess of Sheffield joined her. Their gay laughter rang out as they made for the ballroom's exit.

"You look exceptionally pleased with yourself. Not at all like the sour-faced chap at the Twistleton's musical a few weeks ago."

He tore his gaze from his wife long enough to nod a greeting at Bainbridge. "I'm happier than I deserve."

Unusually reflective, Bainbridge leaned against the column conveniently situated between them. "I wonder if I'll be as fortunate as you, Dandridge, Sutcliffe, and Sheffield. Somehow, I think not. Particularly since you were privileged to pick your duchesses, and mine was chosen for me many years ago. And as my dear mama reminds me on a daily basis, Lady Lilith Brighton is now eight-and-ten. Everyone expects me to set a wedding date."

Sutcliffe approached, champagne in hand. "What's this? Bainbridge, are you contemplating marriage as well?"

"Not by choice, by God," Bainbridge vowed. "Not yet, in any event."

"I've been in search of you all evening," Sutcliffe said. "Westfall wants a word. Something about a horse he wants to acquire."

With a weighty sigh, Bainbridge straightened. "Yes, I think I've located the stud he's been seeking. Oh, and Pennington, so far, I've not been able to find the matched grays you asked me to watch for. I'll let you know if I hear anything."

Max had been trying to find Breckensole's stolen horses for the better part of a month without luck. They'd show up eventually though. A fine pair like that would draw attention and when they did, he intended to recover the team. Not out of any great love for Breckensole. Although, he'd been admirably civilized since Gabriella announced she would marry Max with or without her grandparents' blessing.

Personally, he believed Breckensole had agreed to the quiet ceremony the next day because he truly loved his granddaughter and was absolved from having to part with coin for a formal wedding. That, and if the old curmudgeon cut her off, not so much as a farthing would make its way from Max's purse to Breckensole's.

Though it was boorish of him, Max had no interest in standing up with another lady for a set or two, and instead went in search of the card room. At least that's what he told himself as he wended a path to the exit Gabriella had disappeared through several minutes before.

Once he'd ascended the magnificent curved staircase, he turned right. If memory served, Westfall's private salon and the retiring rooms were along this wing. He contemplated Bainbridge's dilemma as he marched along. Poor sot. An arranged marriage with a child, practically.

Praise God Max had been spared that horror.

A white-gloved feminine hand shot out and grabbed his arm as he passed the salon. "Maxwell," Gabriella whispered, hauling him into the room. "You must see this."

Had she been snooping again? In his four weeks of marriage, he'd learned his darling wife had a curious streak. About more than sexual acts.

She swiftly closed the door and with an impish wink, guided him to the fireplace. Flames burned low in the grate, and a turned down lamp sat upon a side table.

"What exactly is it I'm supposed to be looking at, *chérie*?"

She captured her lower lip between her teeth and pointed to the fur rug before the hearth. "It's fur," she needlessly announced as she removed her gloves.

"Yes?" Max crooked an eyebrow, glancing between her and the thick sable fur. He grinned as comprehension dawned. "Why, Duchess, are you suggesting an erotic assignation on a fur rug during a ball?"

What a wonderfully naughty minx.

"What if I am?" She tilted her chin up.

Chuckling, he locked the door then gathered her into his arms. "I can deny you nothing," he murmured, lowering her to the lush pelt. He leaned over her, brushing a kiss across her rosy lips as he raised her skirts. "You do realize we shall be hopelessly rumpled and wrinkled afterward. Everyone will guess what we've been about."

"We're newly wed." She rolled a shoulder, giving him a sultry look that singed his hair and hardened his groin. "Besides, I don't care if you don't."

She should, and so should he. But damn, he didn't. She reached between them, unfastened his falls, and encircled his sex with her warm hand.

Max groaned, burying his face in her shoulder. "I love you, Gabriella. You are my very life."

"Make love to me, Maxwell," she whispered against his throat before kissing his jaw. "I want to feel you inside me. I want you to give me a child."

And of course he did. In that precise order.

About the Author

USA Today Bestselling, award-winning author COLLETTE CAMERON® scribbles Scottish and Regency historicals featuring dashing rogues and scoundrels and the intrepid damsels who re-form them. Blessed with an overactive and witty muse that won't stop whispering new romantic romps in her ear, she's lived in Oregon her entire life, though she dreams of living in Scotland part-time. A self-confessed Cadbury chocoholic, you'll always find a dash of inspiration and a pinch of humor in her sweet-to-spicy timeless romances®.

Explore **Collette's worlds** at
www.collettecameron.com!

Join her **VIP Reader Club** and **FREE newsletter**.
Giggles guaranteed!

FREE BOOK: Join Collette's The Regency Rose® VIP Reader Club to get updates on book releases, cover reveals, contests and giveaways she reserves exclusively for email and newsletter followers. Also, any deals, sales, or special promotions are offered to club members first. She will not share your name or email, nor will she spam you.

http://bit.ly/TheRegencyRoseGift

Dearest Reader,

Thank you for reading WHAT WOULD A DUKE DO?

I adore stories of redemption, and that's what this story is about. Gabriella and Maxwell learn that love is not enough, but when it is strong and sacrificial, it allows for forgiveness and healing.

The Duke of Bainbridge and Jessica Brentwood's story is next in the series. I'm moving the setting to London for their tale, and what a merry romp it will be.

During the Regency era, any child born within the bounds of matrimony was legally considered progeny of both parents. In the case of the 6th Duke of Pennington, he was forced to acknowledge his wife's child sired by her lover if he wanted the ducal line to continue, as he'd sired no heir himself. Had the child been born outside the bounds of marriage, he would never have been legitimate.

As for the transference of Hartfordshire Court, as the estate wasn't entailed, it could be bought, sold, or even given away. My research also revealed the peculiar window tax which I had never come across before. Obviously, it was a tax geared toward those of means.

Please consider telling other readers why you enjoyed this book by reviewing it. I adore hearing from my readers.

Happy reading!

Collette Cameron

A Diamond for a Duke

SEDUCTIVE SCOUNDRELS SERIES BOOK 1

A dour duke and a wistful wallflower — an impossible match until fate intervenes

Jules, Sixth Duke of Dandridge disdains Society and all its trappings, preferring the country's solitude and peace. Already jaded after the woman he loved died years ago, he's become even more so since unexpectedly inheriting a dukedom's responsibilities and finding himself the target of every husband-hunting vixen in London.

Jemmah Dament has adored Jules from afar for years—since before her family's financial and social reversals. She dares not dream she can win a duke's heart any more than she hopes to escape the life of servitude imposed on her by an uncaring mother. Jemmah knows full well Jules is too far above her station now. Besides, his family has already selected his perfect duchess: a poised, polished, exquisite blueblood.

A chance encounter reunites Jules and Jemmah, resulting in a passionate interlude neither can forget. Jules realizes he wants more—much more—than Jemmah's sweet kisses or her warming his bed. He must somehow convince her to gamble on a dour duke. But can Jemmah trust a man promised to another? One who's sworn never to love again?

Only a Duke Would Dare

SEDUCTIVE SCOUNDRELS SERIES BOOK 2

A reluctant duke. A vicar's daughter. A forbidden love.

Marriage—an unpleasant obligation

A troublesome addendum to his father's will requires Victor, Duke of Sutcliffe to marry before his twenty-seventh birthday or lose his fortune. After a three-year absence, he ventures home, intent upon finding the most biddable and forgettable miss in Essex. A woman who will make no demands upon him and won't mind being left behind when he returns to London. Except, Victor meets Theadosia Brentwood again and finds himself powerless to resist her—even if she is promised to another and the exact opposite of what he thought he wanted in a duchess.

Marriage—an impossible choice

Secretly in love with Victor for years, Theadosia is

overjoyed when he returns. Until she learns he must marry within mere weeks. When he unexpectedly proposes, she must make an impossible decision. How can Thea elope with him when he's marrying out of necessity, not love? Besides, if she does wed Victor, her betrothed—a man she loathes—will reveal a scandalous secret. A secret that will send her father to prison and leave her sister and mother homeless.

A December with a Duke

SEDUCTIVE SCOUNDRELS BOOK 3

He's entirely the wrong sort of man. That's what makes him so utterly *right.*

After a horrific marriage, widow Everleigh Chatterton is cynical and leery of men. She rarely ventures into society, and when she must, she barely speaks to them. Her one regret for refusing to marry again is that she'll never bear children. As a favor to a friend, she reluctantly agrees to attend a Christmas house-party. Unfortunately, Griffin, Duke of Sheffield is also in attendance. Even though Everleigh has previously snubbed him, she can't deny her attraction to the confident, darkly handsome duke.

For almost a year, Griffin has searched for the perfect duchess to help care for the orphan he's taken on. He sets his sights on the exquisite, but unapproachable widow after her sweet interactions with the child impress him. Everleigh vows she's not interested in him or any other man. But Griffin is convinced he can thaw her icy exterior and free the warm, passionate woman lurking behind the arctic facade. Only, as he pursues her, it's his heart that's transformed.

Can Everleigh learn to trust and love again? Will Griffin get his Christmas wish and make her his bride? Or, has he underestimated her wounds and fears and be forced to let her go?

Enjoy the first chapter of

A Diamond for a Duke

Seductive Scoundrels Book One

April 1809

London, England

A pox on duty.

A plague on the pesky dukedom too.

Not the tiniest speck of remorse troubled Jules, Duke of Dandridge as he bolted from the crush of his godmother, Theodora, Viscountess Lockhart's fiftieth birthday ball—without bidding the dear lady a proper farewell, at that.

She'd forgive his discourtesy; his early departure too.

Unlike his mother, his uncles, and the majority of *le beau monde*, Theo understood him.

To honor her, he'd put in a rare social appearance and even stood up for the obligatory dances expected of someone of his station. Through sheer doggedness, he'd also forced his mouth to curve upward—good God, his face ached from the effort—and suffered the toady posturing of husband-stalking mamas and their bevy of pretty, wide-eyed offspring eager to snare an unattached duke.

Noteworthy, considering not so very long ago, Jules scarcely merited a passing glance from the same *tonnish* females now so keen to garner his favor. His perpetual scowl might be attributed to their disinterest.

Tonight's worst offender?

Theo's irksome sister-in-law, Mrs. Dament.

The tenacious woman had neatly maneuvered her admittedly stunning elder daughter, Adelinda, to his side multiple times, and only the Daments' intimate connection to Theo had kept him from turning on his heel at the fourth instance instead of graciously fetching mother and daughter the ratafia they'd requested.

A rather uncouth mental dialogue accompanied his march to the refreshment table, nonetheless.

Where was the other daughter—the sweet-tempered one, Miss Jemmah Dament?

Twiddling her thumbs at home again? Poor, kind, neglected sparrow of a thing.

As children and adolescents, he and Jemmah had been comfortable friends, made so by their similar distressing circumstances. But as must be, they'd grown up, and destiny or fate had placed multiple obstacles between them. He trotted off to university—shortly afterward becoming betrothed to Annabel—and for a time, the Daments simply faded from his and society's notice.

Oh, on occasion, Jules had spied Jemmah in passing. But she'd ducked her shiny honey-colored head and averted her acute sky-blue gaze. Almost as if she was discomfited or he'd somehow offended her.

Yet, after wracking his brain, he couldn't deduce

what his transgression might've been.

At those times, recalling their prior relaxed companionship, his ability to talk to her about anything—or simply remain in compatible silence, an odd twinge pinged behind his ribs. Not regret exactly, though he hardly knew what to label the disquieting sensation.

Quite simply, he missed her friendship and company.

Since Theo's brother, Jasper, died two years ago, Jules had seen little of the Daments.

According to tattle, their circumstances had been drastically reduced. But even so, Jemmah's absence at routs, soirees, and other *ton* gatherings, which her mother and sister often attended, raised questions and eyebrows.

At least arced Jules's brow and stirred his curiosity.

If Jemmah were present at more assemblies, perhaps he'd make more of an effort to put in an appearance.

Or perhaps not.

He held no illusions about his lack of social acumen. A deficiency he had no desire to remedy.

Ever.

A trio of ladies rounded the corner, and he dove into a niche beside a vase-topped table.

The Chinese urn tottered, and he clamped the blue and white china between both hands, lest it crash to the floor and expose him.

He needn't have worried.

So engrossed in their titillating gossip about whether Lord Bacon wore stays, none of the women was the least aware of his presence as they sailed past.

Mentally patting himself on the back for his exceptionally civil behavior for the past pair of vexing hours, Jules permitted a self-satisfied smirk and stepped back into the corridor. He nearly collided with Theo's aged mother-in-law, the Dowager Viscountess Lockhart, come to town for her daughter-in-law's birthday.

A tuft of glossy black ostrich feathers adorned her hair, the tallest of which poked him in the eye.

Hell's bells.

"I beg your pardon, my lady."

Eye watering, Jules grasped her frail elbow, steadying her before she toppled over, such did she sway.

She chuckled, a soft crackle like delicate old lace, and squinted up at him, her faded eyes, the color of weak tea, snapping with mirth.

"Bolting, are you, Dandridge?"

Saucy, astute old bird.

Nothing much escaped Faye, Dowager Viscountess Lockhart's notice.

"I prefer to call it making a prudently-timed departure."

Which he'd be forced to abandon in order to assist the tottering dame back to her preferred throne—*er, seat*—in the ballroom.

He'd congratulated himself prematurely, blast it.

"Allow me to escort you, Lady Lockhart."

He daren't imply she needed his help, or she'd turn her tart tongue, and likely her china-handled cane, on him too.

"Flim flam. Don't be an utter nincompoop. You

mightn't have another opportunity to flee. Go on with you now." She pointed her cane down the deserted passageway. "I'll contrive some drivel to explain your disappearance."

"I don't need a justification."

Beyond that he was bored to his polished shoes, he'd rather munch fresh horse manure than carry on anymore inane conversation, and crowds made him nervous as hell.

Always had.

Hence his infrequent appearances.

Pure naughtiness sparked in the dowager's eyes as she put a bony finger to her chin as if seriously contemplating what shocking tale she'd spin.

"What excuse should I use? Perhaps an abduction? *Hmph*. Not believable." She shook her head, and the ostrich feather danced in agreement. "An elopement? No, no. Won't do at all. Too dull and predictable."

She jutted her finger skyward, nearly poking his other eye.

"Ah, ha! I have just the thing. A scandalous assignation. With a secret love. Oh, yes, that'll do nicely."

A decidedly teasing smile tipped her thin lips.

Jules vacillated.

She was right, of course.

If he didn't make good his escape now, he mightn't be able to for hours. Still, his conscience chafed at leaving her to hobble her way to the ballroom alone. For all of his darkling countenance and brusque comportment, he was still a gentleman first.

Lady Lockhart extracted her arm, and then poked him in the bicep with her pointy nail.

Hard.

"Go, I said, young scamp." Only she would dare call a duke a scamp. "I assure you, I'm not so infirm that I'm incapable of walking the distance without tumbling onto my face."

Maybe not her face, but what about the rest of her feeble form?

Her crepey features softened, and the beauty she'd once been peeked through the ravages of age. "It was good of you to come, Dandridge, and I know it meant the world to Theodora." The imp returned full on, and she bumped her cane's tip against his instep. "Now git yourself gone."

"Thank you, my lady." Jules lifted her hand, and after kissing the back, waited a few moments to assess her progress. If she struggled the least, he'd lay aside his plans and disregard her command.

A few feet along the corridor, she paused, half-turning toward him. Starchy silvery eyebrow raised, she mouthed, "Move your arse."

With a sharp salute, Jules complied and continued to reflect on his most successful venture into society in a great while.

Somehow—multiple glasses of superb champagne might be attributed to helping—he'd even managed to converse—perhaps a little less courteously than the majority of attendees, but certainly not as tersely as he was generally wont to—with the young bucks, dandies, and past-their-prime decrepitudes whose trivial interests consisted of horseflesh, the preposterous wagers on White's books, and the next bit of feminine fluff they might sample.

Or, in the older, less virile coves' cases, the

unfortunate woman subjected to their lusty ogling since the aged chaps' softer parts were wont to stay that way.

Only the welcome presence of the two men whom Jules might truly call 'friend,' Maxwell, Duke of Pennington, and Victor, Duke of Sutcliffe, had made the evening, if not pleasant, undoubtedly more interesting with their barbed humor and ongoing litany of drolly murmured sarcastic observations.

Compared to that acerbic pair, Jules, renowned for his acute intellect and grave mien, seemed quite the epitome of frivolous jollity.

But, by spitting camels, when his uncles, Leopold and Darius—from whom his middle names had been derived—had cornered him in the card room and demanded to know for the third time this month when he intended to do his *ducal duty*?

Marry and produce an heir...

Damn their interfering eyes!

Jules's rigidly controlled temper had slipped loose of its moorings, and he'd told them—ever so calmly, but also enunciating each syllable most carefully lest the mulish, bacon-brained pair misunderstand a single word—"go bugger yourselves and leave me be!"

He'd been officially betrothed once and nearly so a second time in his five-and-twenty years. Never again.

Never?

Fine, maybe someday. But not to a Society damsel and not for many, *many* years or before *he* had concluded the parson's mousetrap was both necessary and convenient. Should that fateful day never come to pass, well, best his Charmont uncles get busy producing male heirs themselves instead of dallying with actresses and opera singers.

Marching along the corridor, Jules tipped his mouth into his first genuine smile since alighting from his coach, other than the one he'd bestowed upon Theo when he arrived. Since his affianced, Annabel's death five years ago, Theo was one of the few people he felt any degree of true affection for.

Must be a character flaw—an inadequacy in his emotional reservoir, this inability to feel earnest emotions. In any event, he wanted to return home early enough to bid his niece and ward, Lady Sabrina Remington, good-night as he'd promised.

They'd celebrated her tenth birthday earlier today, too.

Jules truly enjoyed Sabrina's company.

Possibly because he could simply be himself, not Duke of Dandridge, or a peer, or a member of the House of Lords. Not quarry for eager-to-wed chits, a tolerant listener of friends' ribald jokes, or a wise counselor to troubled acquaintances. Not even a dutiful nephew, a less-favored son, a preferred godson, or at one time, a loving brother and wholly-devoted intended.

Anticipation of fleeing the crowd lengthening his strides, he cut a swift glance behind him, and his gut plummeted, arse over chin, to his shiny shoes.

Blisters and ballocks.

Who the devil invited *her*?

Made in the USA
Monee, IL
14 August 2021

75671719R00193